Jane's bottom l
know how I got
were the one who found me. If it had been anyone else, my face would be plastered all over town."

"I don't think so." Rob raised her hand to his lips and kissed the tips of her fingers, immediately regretting it.

He loosened his clasp on her hand, but she curled her fingers around his thumb.

"Why stop?" Her whispered words echoed in his head, as if they'd come from his own brain.

"You know why. It's not a good idea for us..."

"It seems like a really good idea to me right now. You're my anchor, Rob."

"I'm your only acquaintance. Of course you're going to feel this way about me." He traced the curve of her neck with his fingertip. "You want comfort. I understand. It must be scary as hell to be where you are right now. I get it."

Turning her head, she pressed a kiss on his palm. "I don't think you get it at all, Rob..."

UNRAVELING JANE DOE

CAROL ERICSON

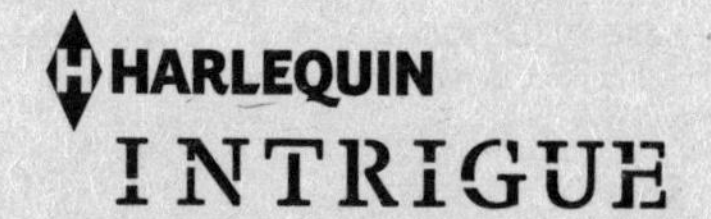

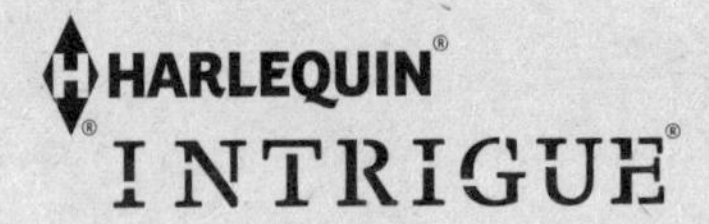

Recycling programs for this product may not exist in your area.

ISBN-13: 978-1-335-13592-6

Unraveling Jane Doe

This edition published by arrangement with Harlequin Books S.A.

For questions and comments about the quality of this book, please contact us at CustomerService@Harlequin.com.

Harlequin Enterprises ULC
22 Adelaide St. West, 40th Floor
Toronto, Ontario M5H 4E3, Canada
www.Harlequin.com

Printed in U.S.A.

Carol Ericson is a bestselling, award-winning author of more than forty books. She has an eerie fascination for true-crime stories, a love of film noir and a weakness for reality TV, all of which fuel her imagination to create her own tales of murder, mayhem and mystery. To find out more about Carol and her current projects, please visit her website at www.carolericson.com, "where romance flirts with danger."

Books by Carol Ericson

Harlequin Intrigue

Holding the Line

Evasive Action
Chain of Custody
Unraveling Jane Doe

Red, White and Built: Delta Force Deliverance

Enemy Infiltration
Undercover Accomplice
Code Conspiracy

Red, White and Built: Pumped Up

Delta Force Defender
Delta Force Daddy
Delta Force Die Hard

Red, White and Built

Locked, Loaded and SEALed
Alpha Bravo SEAL
Bullseye: SEAL
Point Blank SEAL
Secured by the SEAL
Bulletproof SEAL

Her Alibi

Harlequin Intrigue Noir

Toxic

Visit the Author Profile page at Harlequin.com.

CAST OF CHARACTERS

Jane Doe/Libby James—A crash survivor with no memory, she soon realizes the more she remembers, the more she puts herself in danger, but she's forced to keep secrets from the only man who can help her.

Rob Valdez—When this Border Patrol agent comes across a crash scene and a woman with amnesia, his protective instincts kick into overdrive, but Jane Doe pushes him away with her secrets—secrets that might be the death of them both.

Troy Paulsen—A private investigator on the verge of solving the biggest case of his career is halted by his informant's memory loss… He'll do anything to get her to remember.

Pablo Bustamante—This stranger comes out of the woodwork claiming to be Jane's husband, but his intentions are less than honorable.

April Archer—A Border Patrol agent's wife, she has a vested interest in finding out the identity of El Gringo Viejo, and a woman with no memory might be her only hope.

El Gringo Viejo—A notorious and mysterious drug supplier in Mexico, he wants Jane Doe dead before she can ID him.

Chapter One

The smell of burning rubber assailed her nose and woke her with a jolt. Her head snapped up. Pain seared through her skull.

Her eyelids flew open. She blinked at the upside-down tree.

She clenched her teeth at the sound of a wheel spinning around and around, squealing with every turn. Her jaw throbbed.

The seat belt dug into her neck, and she reached down to tug on it. Her fingers crawled to the side of her head to probe the area that screamed with pain. The tips slid through strands of sticky hair.

She pulled her hand away and held it in front of her face. She tried to focus on the red streaks running down her arm. Blood. Her blood.

She swallowed and gagged. Swallowing and hanging upside down had its difficulties. She snorted out a laugh. People stuck on an amusement park ride must feel something like this—only this was no amusement park.

Her hand followed her seat belt to the latch. If she released too quickly, her head would bang against the roof of the car. It already hurt like hell. She didn't need any more injuries.

She braced one hand on the roof of the vehicle and unsnapped the seat belt with her other hand. Her body slumped and curled in on itself in a fetal position as she rolled to her side.

She felt for the car door handle, but when she reached it, the handle wouldn't release. Her fingers scrabbled to find the button for the door locks, and she clicked them open. She tried the handle again. This time, the door opened but not all the way. Repositioning herself, she shoved at the door with her feet, the edge of it scraping through dirt and sand.

When just enough of a space opened, she started to slither through it. Voices above her caused her to freeze with her feet just outside the car.

A man's voice carried through the air, over the sound of the spinning wheel. "Should we go down?"

Another man answered him in accented English. "What do you think? I haven't seen a thing move since it crashed."

Terror seized her. Their words, their tone,

their *something* pumped adrenaline through her system, revving up her sluggish, aching body.

She wriggled the rest of the way through the car door and crouched in the dirt beside the mangled, upended car. It lay at the bottom of a gully on the desert floor.

She peered over the top of the wreck at the ridge above and at two pairs of boots standing at the edge. The owners of those boots couldn't see her, and for some reason, she wanted to make sure they never did.

One pair of boots, black with silver tips that glinted in the sun, made a move, and several pebbles tumbled down the embankment.

The owner of the boots said, "We have to be certain."

"You go, man. I'm not going down there. What if the car explodes?"

"I'd rather be in a car explosion than face El Gringo Viejo and tell him we're not sure she's dead."

"I have an idea. You see that gasoline leaking?"

The smell of gasoline now permeated her nose. Why hadn't she noticed it before? The car could've gone up in flames at any time.

"Give me the cigarette, *cabron*. You're too chicken to get close enough."

If she ran now, they'd see her. Better to let

them think she'd gone up in flames with the car. She coiled her body, her muscles quivering.

A few more pebbles rolled down as the man with the silver-tipped black boots ventured down the embankment sideways. He stopped, and she held her breath.

The other man laughed from above. "You missed."

Two seconds later, a fire whipped up on the other side of the car. Fueled by the gasoline, it roared to life.

Using the flames and smoke as cover, she crawled through the sand toward that upside-down tree she'd spied through the cracked windshield, now right-side up. Leaning against its rough bark, she drew her knees to her chest, willing herself to shrink into the bark. Willing the two men to stay away.

When the car exploded, a door sailed past her and black smoke billowed into the blue cloudless sky. She stayed put, folding her arms across her body, fingers digging into her biceps.

A hot breeze carried the two male voices toward her, but she couldn't make out their words this time over the crackling blaze. She squeezed her eyes shut and mumbled to herself, "Go away. Go away."

A car started—maybe not. A small explosion sent another flurry of debris skyward, and she covered her nose and mouth with her hands to block out the acrid smoke and ash.

Her head hurt. Her lungs hurt. Her ribs hurt. And still she sat. She sat as the car burned out behind her. She sat as a lizard skittered across her toes. She sat as the sun dipped behind the hills. She sat as feral eyes glowed at her through the darkness.

Finally, her muscles stiff and her throat parched, she peeled herself away from the tree and cranked her head around. Wisps of smoke still rose from the torched husk of the car. It crouched in the desert like some watchful creature.

She patted the pockets of her pants and pulled out a few pesos from the front and a knife with a fancy handle from the back. She hit the button on the side of the knife, and a shiny blade materialized. She just might need that. She retracted the blade and shoved it back into her pocket, stepping away from the tree and scanning the ground.

The light from the half-moon provided scant illumination, but she spotted some debris in the sand. She squatted and picked through some scraps of paper, empty cigarette packages, receipts and bits of paper and plastic bags.

She snatched up one piece of paper stirring in the faint breeze and flattened it out on her knee.

Someone had sketched the face of a man with longish hair and glasses—just more trash. She swept it from her leg and scanned the ground for something useful.

The desert floor stared back at her with hooded eyes, giving up nothing.

She glanced up at the ridge where the two men had stood and discussed her demise. They'd probably left hours ago, but fear had kept her attached to that tree. She needed a way out of here, water, food.

But most of all, she needed to find out who she was.

Rob climbed into his Border Patrol truck and slumped behind the wheel, leaving his door open. He massaged his temples and whispered, "What a day."

The hushed voice came from a place of reverence for the desert and its undercover creatures. He could shout at the top of his lungs and no human soul would hear him.

He sat for a moment, his hands resting on the steering wheel, soaking in the peacefulness. As a Border Patrol agent, he knew this stretch of the desert didn't always host serenity. He'd experienced firsthand the headless bodies, the shoot-outs and the drugs—always the drugs.

His fingers curled around the steering wheel.

Drugs had ravaged his life. They didn't represent some inanimate object to him. He viewed drugs as some great evil that had become his personal enemy.

He'd never expressed it quite like that when he'd applied for a job with the Border Patrol. The agency probably would've dismissed him based on his psych eval if he had.

He loosened his death grip on the steering wheel and ran a hand through his hair. He didn't want to pollute the evening with thoughts of home.

Easing the door of his truck closed, he started the engine. The sound would scatter all the shy creatures and maybe even a drug dealer or two, although his survey of the border today probably already did that.

He buzzed down his window and wheeled the truck around. The truck bumped along the dirt of the access road until it hit the asphalt, which didn't provide a much smoother ride. He flicked on his brights. He didn't want to mow down anything out here, and it wouldn't be likely that he'd be blinding another driver at this time of night.

The warm breeze from the window caressed his face, and he inhaled the scents from the desert, subtle but distinct. His nostrils flared at an alien odor.

Despite the hot and dry conditions of the Sonoran Desert, fires didn't commonly occur due to the lack of combustible vegetation, but he'd definitely caught a whiff of burning rubber and gasoline. He pulled over and adjusted his rearview mirror, studying the landscape behind him.

The road had crested and the desert floor had fallen away, down a steep embankment. Scanning the space to the side of the road, Rob detected a stream of gray smoke curling toward the sky.

He threw the truck into Reverse and backed onto the shoulder, giving himself plenty of space between his tires and the edge of the ridge that fell away about fifteen feet.

He left his headlights on and grabbed the flashlight from his truck. He exited his vehicle, planting his boots on the shifting gravel. Peering over the side of the road, he aimed his flashlight in the area where he'd seen the smoke.

The beam of light picked out the skeleton of a car, burned down to bare bones. "Damn."

Torched cars did occasionally appear in this part of the desert. Sometimes car thieves dumped the fruits of their labor here after stripping them of usable parts. Sometimes coyotes got rid of their vehicles after transporting their human cargo across the border. And sometimes people had accidents.

Rob edged sideways down the embankment, wedging his boots in the dirt and rock with each step. He called out for the hell of it. "Anyone here?"

If anyone had been in that car, he or she would've perished in the fire. The car hadn't crashed that recently, so even if someone had survived the impact and the inferno, that person probably wouldn't have survived exposure to these harsh elements.

When he reached the car, he kicked at the frame with the toe of his boot. It collapsed with a squeal. Walking around the vehicle, he searched for the VIN, license plate and any other type of identifying information. He couldn't even tell what kind of car it had been.

As he turned toward the embankment leading back up to the road, a rustling sound stopped him in his tracks. He glanced over his shoulder. It could be anything.

He eyed the paloverde tree and a few scrubby bushes to the right of the car. He'd probably startled an animal holing up there. Running his flashlight over the vegetation, he squinted at the outlines of the tree's low branches. Something bigger than a longhorn sheep could be hiding out there, something as big as a person.

"Hello?" He started walking toward the tree. "Anyone there?"

Something decidedly human coughed, and a shape emerged from behind the tree.

"Are you all right? Is that your car?" He swept the beam of his flashlight over the figure.

A woman stepped forward, blinking in the light. She raised her arm, her hand gripping a knife, and said, "Take one more step and I'll gut you."

Chapter Two

Rob stumbled back, the light from the flashlight crisscrossing over the woman's body. His hand hovered over his gun holstered in his belt. He couldn't shoot an accident victim. She'd probably lost her senses out here alone.

His gaze darted past her. She *was* alone, wasn't she? Maybe he'd walked into some sort of ambush.

He flexed his fingers near the butt of his .45. "I'm not going to hurt you. Are you injured? Is that your car?"

"I'm fine. You can keep moving." She flashed the knife, and it glinted in his beam of light.

She'd clearly lost it. "Keep moving? No way. You're not fine. You're a bloody mess."

She touched her hair, clumped with blood, and then drew back her shoulders. "It's nothing."

"Look, ma'am, you don't have to be afraid. I'm a Border Patrol agent. My truck's on the road above." He jerked his thumb over his shoulder in case she'd forgotten the direction of the road.

"Border Patrol? What border?" Her eyes gleamed in the dark like some feral creature's.

He pulled his badge and ID from his pocket and extended his hand toward her. "Mexican border."

He couldn't tell in this light if she were Latina. Could that car have belonged to a coyote transporting people across the border? That would explain her skittishness. She didn't have an accent, but that didn't mean anything.

She darted forward and snatched the ID from his hand. Cupping it in her palm, she squinted at it.

He aimed his flashlight at her hand so she could see his ID.

She read aloud, "'Roberto Valdez.'"

He raised his right hand. "That's me. I can take you to the hospital right now, or if you don't want to ride with me, I can call the police, an ambulance."

"No cops." She threw the billfold containing his badge and ID back at him. It landed at his feet. "No cops. No ambulance. No hospital. I'm fine."

"Ma'am, I can't leave you out here. You'll die. It's miles from the nearest town. There's a hodgepodge collection of campers and RVs closer than town, but it's not safe there."

"I'm not going with you to the cops or hospital." She dropped the knife and put a hand to her throat. "Please. I—I don't think I'd be safe there."

He tilted his head. "Why not? Did you come across the border illegally? Did a coyote bring you?"

"What? No." She shook her head, and the tangled strands of her hair whipped back and forth. "Nothing like that. Please. I-it's my husband, my ex-husband. He's after me, and I'm afraid."

Rob swallowed. If she just lied to him, she'd picked the best lie to tug at his heartstrings.

He waved his arm toward the burned-out car. "Did he do this?"

"I think so. I think he caused the accident and then made sure the car went up in flames."

"Why didn't you go up in flames with it?"

"After the accident, I saw him coming for me, so I hid behind the tree and clump of bushes. He set the car on fire and took off. He never saw me. He thinks I'm dead, and I want to keep it that way."

"If we call the police..."

"No cops!" She dipped down and scooped up the knife. "I swear, you'll have to shoot me with that gun you keep touching, or I'll run off into the desert and you can forget you ever saw me."

"I'm not going to shoot you, but I'm not going to let you run away, either. What's your name?"

"J-Jane."

He narrowed his eyes. Blatant lie. "Last name?"

"Doesn't matter."

"Okay… Jane." He held out his hand. "I'm Rob Valdez, and I'm gonna help you out."

She folded her arms. "Not by taking me to the hospital and calling the police. That's not going to help me."

"We'll figure something out. Let's get you out of this desert. I have water in the truck." Locking his gaze with hers, he ducked to pick up his badge and ID.

"Water?" Her body swayed to the side and she braced a hand against a branch of the paloverde tree.

"That's right. You must be parched." He inched closer to her, shuffling his boots in the sand.

"Water?" As the word left her lips, she crumpled to the ground.

Rob lunged forward. He placed one foot on top of the knife, driving it into the dirt just in case this was some kind of scam.

He crouched next to her and whistled as he touched the wound on the side of her head. No scam.

He swept his light across the ground to see

if she had anything besides the knife and the clothes on her back. She didn't.

He pocketed the knife, placed the flashlight between his teeth and slid his arms beneath Jane's lithe frame. He pushed up, clasping her to his chest, and picked his way over the ground.

Trooping up the incline carrying dead weight, even though that dead weight was as light as a feather, was proving to be a challenge. He pumped his legs, digging his feet into the sand with each step. When he reached the top, he placed Jane on the ground and scrambled over the ridge. He scooped her up again and placed her in the passenger seat of the truck, snapping the seat belt across her body. He reclined the seat and checked her vitals.

He wouldn't call her pulse strong, but it beat steadily beneath his fingers. Her parched lips parted, and she released a soft sigh. Her dark lashes fluttered.

He held his breath, willing her to come to. He'd rather have her conscious and threatening him with that knife than out like this.

Reaching into the back seat, he grabbed the first-aid kit every Border Patrol vehicle carried. He flipped it open and snagged some gauze and antiseptic from two compartments. He lifted the top tray and pinched a clean cloth between two fingers. He soaked it with water from his bottle and dabbed the cut on Jane's head. Head wounds always bled all out of proportion to their seriousness, but this nasty gash had him worried.

He should just drive her straight to the hospital and let a professional take care of her. Even if her ex found her out, the cops could protect her.

His hands froze and he snorted. He knew better than anyone the fallacy of that misplaced belief. He finished cleaning the dried blood from her cut and applied some antiseptic.

Her breath quickened and her eyelids squeezed tighter.

"Jane?" he whispered in her ear, but it probably wouldn't do much good. If her name was Jane, his was Tarzan.

He wrapped some gauze around her head like a hippie headband to cover the injury in case her movement caused it to bleed again. Then he dumped some water on another clean cloth and pressed it against her lips.

She moaned and shifted in her seat.

"I've got you. You're safe. Wake up and drink some water."

She mumbled something and moved her arm.

"That's it. Come out of it."

Her eyes flew open, and she stared at him. Panic flooded her face. She jerked forward against the seat belt and lurched back against the restraint.

"You're all right. You're all right. Remember? I'm Border Patrol agent Rob Valdez. You passed out down there, and now you're in my truck."

Her hands flailed for a few seconds. "No police."

"I didn't call the police. I didn't call anyone." He held out the bottle of water. "I cleaned your wound. I did the best I could, but..."

"No hospital." She shook her head, gasped and then cradled one side of her face with her palm.

"Okay, no hospital, either, but you need to take it easy." He held the water to her lips. "Drink. You're dehydrated."

Closing her eyes, she gulped back the water, finishing almost half of the liquid. She shoved the bottle between her knees and wrapped both hands around it, denting the plastic.

Rob cleared his throat. "Is there someplace I can drop you? A friend? Relative? Bus station? I can drive you up to Tucson, if you like."

She opened one eye. "Tucson?"

"Isn't that where you were headed when you had the crash?" He'd just assumed that. *Jane* hadn't told him a whole helluva lot outside of the story of her abusive ex. He tilted his head.

"Where were you headed? How'd you wreck that car?"

He should've been asking these questions before he got her in his truck.

"I wasn't running toward anything or anyone." She put a hand to her throat, and her voice hitched. "I was just running away."

"You don't have any friends or relatives in this area? No bags? No money? No car?"

"Everything burned up in that inferno." She swept her hair, clumped with blood, from her cheek where a single tear sparkled. "I'm so tired, so weak."

Rob patted her knee and pushed up to his feet. What kind of brute was he, interrogating her on this desert road when she needed food and meds and rest?

"I can take you back to my place for now, so you can get your bearings. Is that all right?"

"How's your family going to feel about it? I don't want to put anyone out."

"I don't have a family—at least not one I live with. If you'd rather stay with a family, I can probably drop you off with my buddy and his wife." He scratched his chin. "I *think* that would be okay."

Whom was he kidding? Clay Archer played by the rules, even if his wife, April, didn't. Clay would call the cops for sure.

"Your buddy? Is he a Border Patrol agent, like you?"

"He is."

She held out a hand. "That's okay. I trust you. I mean, you rescued me. I just need a day to regroup."

"Of course, yeah, regroup. I have more water at my place and some leftover food, and even some ibuprofen, which seems to be missing from my first-aid kit."

He closed the door of the truck and went around to the driver's side. Sliding behind the wheel, he glanced at the petite woman in the seat next to him, her dark lashes creating two perfect crescents on her cheeks.

Maybe it would be better if he didn't call his coworkers on this one. They were always telling him how impulsive he was, and this would give them more ammunition.

He studied Jane's profile, convinced she was faking sleep, and started the truck.

The woman had to be about a 110 soaking wet. He'd feed her, let her get some rest and get her bearings.

How much trouble could she be?

THE BORDER PATROL AGENT... Rob...prodded her shoulder. "Are you awake? Conscious?"

She stretched her arms and rubbed her eyes.

She'd been awake the whole way but didn't want to face any more of his questions. How could she? She didn't have any answers.

She'd learned she was somewhere between the Mexican border and Tucson, but how she got here, she hadn't a clue. Scratch that. She'd been driving that car when it crashed. She hadn't even thought to grab anything from the car before she scrambled out of it.

Now she had nothing…except that knife, which he'd taken. She slid a gaze at the earnest young man beside her. Well, nothing except this hot Latino with his soulful dark eyes and ready sympathy.

"Feeling any better?"

"Not much." She clapped a hand on the back of her neck and twisted her head from side to side. "I'm feeling stiff."

"This is my place." He pointed out the windshield as they pulled into the driveway of a small house with lights burning in the front windows. "I'll get you some ice, ibuprofen, food and water—in whatever order you want—and then you can make your plans in the morning."

"Water, pain meds and ice first." She finished off the bottle of water still clutched in her hands. Her plans for the morning swam in her head in a misty fog with all the other confusing thoughts—including her identity.

Jane—what an idiot. Why didn't she just call herself Jane Doe? Rob didn't believe her for a second. What else hadn't he believed?

At least he hadn't run to the cops. She'd felt sure a Border Patrol agent would be duty-bound to call the police and report the accident and its strange victim.

His face had softened when she'd told him the story about the violent ex-husband. She cringed a little inside when she saw how her lie had affected him… But it could be the truth.

Maybe one of those men who'd planned to kill her by setting fire to the car was an ex. She couldn't remember their words right now, but they'd come to her later—unless she had some sort of weird short-term memory loss where she couldn't remember even recent events.

She remembered Rob Valdez, though, and his kindness. Her gaze flicked over him. And the way that shirt from his green uniform hugged his shoulders and tightened across his chest when he moved. She couldn't be too messed up if she could still appreciate a handsome man in uniform.

She jumped when he put his hand on her arm. His touch sent some sort of electric current through her system, or it made her nervous.

He snatched his hand back. "I'm sorry. Did I hurt you?"

"No. I'm still on edge."

"If you're nervous about coming into my house, I can check with my coworker and his wife. You might feel more comfortable there."

She doubted she'd feel more comfortable with another Border Patrol agent. She couldn't possibly get lucky a second time with a law enforcement official who wouldn't run straight to the cops.

"It's not that. I'm still nervous about my ex… and what he did to me." As she threw that last bit in there, Rob's eyes turned into liquid velvet. His pumped-up frame housed a soft heart—and she had to take advantage of that soft heart right now, no matter how wretched it made her feel.

He snatched his keys from the ignition, and all that softness morphed into hard lines and a clenched jaw. "I can imagine, but you'll be safe here."

And she believed him—not only that she'd be safe with him but that he *could* imagine. Of course, what did she know? How could she read people when she couldn't remember any people in her own life?

"I'll help you out." He clambered from the truck with his equipment belt squeaking and a backpack slung over one shoulder.

By the time he came around to her side of the truck, she'd unlatched her seat belt and grabbed on to the water bottle—her single possession at this point besides her dirty and tattered clothing.

He opened the door and held out his hand. “Hang on.”

She did hold on to his hand while he guided her out of the truck and walked her up to his house. The blue door with the light above it stood out against the beige stucco of the house. The door fitted into an arched entryway that led to a courtyard with potted cactus and chairs gathered around a wood-burning potbellied stove. He wouldn’t have need of that during what must be summer.

She placed a hand over her heart. She didn’t even know the season, but the intense heat marked it for summer.

“Are you all right?”

“You’re a kind person.”

A flush edged into his face just beneath his mocha skin, and he snorted. “Kind? Okay.”

They crossed the courtyard, and he unlocked the front door. The tile floors and adobe walls created a cool cocoon, and she released a long breath.

Rob dropped his stuff on a bench in the foyer and brushed past her as he strode into the living room. He gathered some throw pillows on the couch and bunched them up on one side. As he patted the cushion, he said, "Sit right here. I'll get you some cold water and ice for your head."

She sank to the couch, propping her arm on top of the pillows. "Can I use your restroom?"

"Of course." He smacked his forehead with the heel of his hand. "What am I thinking? Second door on your right down the hall. Do you need help?"

"I think I can make it." She rose to her feet and headed for the hallway. She pushed open the door of the bathroom and held her breath as she squared herself in front of the mirror.

She sucked in a breath at the reflection that stared back at her. She flicked a strand of light brown hair as her brown eyes surveyed the unfamiliar face. No, not unfamiliar. Had there been a spark of recognition at the unexceptional features? Brown hair, brown eyes, slightly upturned nose. Nothing that would make her stand out in a crowd—she liked that.

She patted the clumped hair on the side of her head and gritted her teeth as she traced the bandage Rob had wrapped around her head.

He tapped on the door. "Everything okay?"

Oh, yeah. Just getting acquainted with my face.

Inserting a finger beneath the gauze, she said, "Should we take off this bandage?"

"I can replace that with something better.

I have a whole first-aid station out here when you're ready."

She flung open the door and he jerked back. "I'm ready."

"Worse than you expected?" He cocked his head.

"Better, a lot better." She followed him into the living room and took her place in the little nest he'd fashioned for her on one side of the couch.

He'd arrayed bottles, bandages, water and an ice pack on the coffee table in front of her.

"Let's replace that bandage. I can do a better job now." He sat beside her and unwound the gauze from her head. He dabbed the edge of a wet towel on her wound, cleaning more blood from her scalp.

As he applied more antiseptic, she flinched.

"Sorry."

When he finished with the bandage, he offered her two ibuprofen cupped in his palm. She downed them with the water.

"Now you need some food."

Her gaze shifted from his face to the small kitchen behind him. "Don't go to any trouble."

"You won't let me take you to the hospital. I can't let you starve." He jumped up and swept up several items from the table. "No trouble, either. I have some leftover albondigas soup and half a turkey sandwich I swear I didn't touch."

"That sounds good, but what are you eating?" She would've killed for a sandwich this afternoon, but she'd gotten used to the hunger clawing at her stomach.

As he walked into the kitchen, he glanced over his shoulder. "I ate dinner hours ago. You do realize it's almost midnight?"

She didn't know much, but she'd noticed the time when she got into his truck. It had been light outside when the car crashed.

"Just want to make sure I'm not stealing your leftovers."

"Not at all." He ducked into the fridge and pulled out a bag with one hand and a plastic container with the other. He tipped the container of the soup back and forth. "I'll heat this up."

She toed off her canvas shoes, dirty and filled with sand, and curled one leg beneath her. Releasing a long breath, she relaxed her shoulders for probably the first time since she'd awakened in that car. She didn't want to think about tomorrow. Didn't want to think about who she was and why two men were trying to kill her.

The beep of the microwave penetrated her thoughts, and she sat forward, her mouth watering at the spicy aroma of the soup.

After clinking around in the kitchen for a few

minutes, Rob emerged carrying a tray. He set it on the coffee table in front of her and even shook out the cloth napkin and placed it on her lap.

"What service, but I feel guilty." She waved a spoon at him.

"Don't worry about me." He backtracked to the kitchen and grabbed a bottle of beer from the fridge and twisted off the cap. "This is all I need right now. It had been a rough day even before I spied your car off the road."

She paused in the middle of stirring the soup, the little whirlpool in the liquid mimicking her mind. "You saw the crash from the road?"

"I saw the smoke. I know that piece of desert like the back of my hand." He took a swig of beer. "I'd offer you one, but I don't think alcohol is a good idea in your condition."

He had no idea. "Don't think so, either. Water's fine."

"Can I ask you what happened out there? Was someone chasing you? You lost control?" He'd sat down in the chair across from her, rolling the bottle between his hands.

"Yes." She blew on a spoonful of soup. Better to stay as close to the truth as possible.

"Did your ex see the car go over?"

"I think so." She pressed two fingers against her throbbing temple. "I don't remember that much about the crash and the aftermath."

"And he just left you there?" Rob dragged a fingernail through the damp label on his bottle. "Damn."

"He must have." She lifted one shoulder and slurped up some soup.

"Where were you coming from? Where do you live?"

She squeezed her eyes closed. "I'd rather not talk about it. Is that okay?"

"Sure, sure." He tipped his head. "How's the soup?"

"Delicious." She scooped up another spoonful of veggies and tasty broth. "Did you make this?"

"No. A woman who owns a restaurant in town always makes up a batch for me because I told her it was just like my *abuela*'s."

"Are you from… Tucson?"

"LA, originally." His hand tightened on the beer bottle for a second. "I moved to Paradiso when I got hired on with the Border Patrol."

"Paradiso?"

"That's the town we're in now. You must've seen the signs for it on the road up from…wherever."

She nodded so hard, a shaft of pain skewered her skull. She pushed the soup aside and dug into the sandwich. Maybe if she kept her mouth full, Rob wouldn't ask her any more questions.

He let her eat in peace as he finished his beer,

and when she popped the last of the sandwich into her mouth, he made a move for the tray.

Putting a hand on his arm, she said, "I'll do it. I need to move from this spot."

"If you say so." He carried his empty bottle into the kitchen.

She pushed up from the couch and dropped her napkin onto the plate. Then she reached up to stretch and bent over the coffee table to pick up the tray.

Rob called from the kitchen. "Who's Rosalinda?"

She almost sent the dishes crashing down. "What?"

He reached behind him and rubbed his back. "That tattoo on your back. Who's Rosalinda?"

Chapter Three

She froze, gripping the tray with both hands, wanting to drop it and tug down her shirt. Instead she composed her expression, popped up and spun around. "Sh-she was a friend of mine who died. All of us, her particular friends, got her name tattooed on our backs."

"That's quite a tribute."

"She was murdered." She snapped her mouth shut. Why was she throwing out all these details? It might make her story more believable but easier to debunk—not that Rob Valdez would be debunking anything about her. She'd be out of his wavy, dark hair tomorrow.

"I'm sorry." He parked himself in front of the sink and rinsed out the plastic soup container.

The air crackled between them. She knew he had questions on his lips, but he knew by now she'd shut him down.

Was her name Rosalinda? Did people tattoo their own names on their bodies?

She delivered the tray to the kitchen, and he snatched the dishes from it and ran them under the water.

"I have three bedrooms in this place. One of the extra rooms is an office and the other is a spare bedroom. You're welcome to sleep there. The door has a lock on it."

Leaning her back against the counter, she folded her hands behind her. "I trust you."

His eyebrows quirked over his nose for a split second. "You shouldn't be so trusting."

"Of you?" She pressed a hand against her stomach. Had she totally misread Rob Valdez? Being in law enforcement didn't automatically make him a good guy. Maybe he'd been so accommodating about not calling the police because he wanted to…take advantage of her in some way. Who knew he had her here? Nobody.

"Sorry." He grabbed a dish towel and waved it in the air like a white flag. "I didn't mean to freak you out. You have nothing to worry about from me. I'm just saying, in general, you've been very trusting tonight—except for the part where you pulled a knife on me."

"Not putting my faith in anyone all day almost got me killed out there in the desert. I figured if I were going to trust anyone, it would be a Border Patrol agent."

"That makes sense. I'm glad it was me."

"Me, too." And she wasn't even talking about the way his shirt stretched across the muscles of his back as he washed the dishes, or even the fact that he was washing dishes. Rob Valdez possessed a calmness that inspired the same in her. She didn't know who she was or who was after her, she'd survived a car crash and a day in the desert without food or water, and yet she'd managed to chow down some food and felt ready for bed…sleep.

"Can I—" she plucked the blood-and-dirt-stained T-shirt from her body "—shower?"

"I'll get you a towel and one of my T-shirts. If you want to give me your stuff, I can stick it in the washing machine." He reached out and tugged on the hem of her ripped shirt. "Can't do much about that."

That rip had exposed the tattoo on her back, but at least it had given her a clue to her identity. Maybe she'd wake up tomorrow morning and remember everything. Maybe she had a frantic husband or boyfriend somewhere.

Her gaze slid to Rob, still in possession of her T-shirt. Then she'd end this interlude and be on her merry way. Merry way with two guys out to kill her?

Tomorrow morning, she'd try to remember what they'd said, but now she just wanted sleep.

"I'll probably just toss it when I get…home,

but yeah, putting on some clean clothes tomorrow would help a lot."

He released the shirt, a flush rising from his chest. "I'll get that towel. You can use the same bathroom you were in before."

"Thanks. I really appreciate everything you've done tonight. You didn't have to do anything, especially when I brandished that knife at you."

"I couldn't leave you there, and that knife?" He winked at her. "I could've disarmed you and taken you down at any time."

He pivoted and exited the kitchen. She watched his departure through narrowed eyes, his broad shoulders and pumped-up arms lending truth to his claim. Despite his caring nature and surface geniality, it would be a mistake to underestimate Rob.

She dried the dishes he'd left in the dish drainer and was putting away the last one when he returned.

"You didn't have to do that."

"I'm not as bad off as I look. I was wearing my seat belt."

"But the car was upside down, wasn't it? I could tell that even from its condition." He shook his head. "You're lucky to be alive."

She shivered and folded her arms. "I am."

He gestured behind him. "I put a towel and

one of my T-shirts in that bathroom. There's soap and shampoo, if you think you can wash around the bandage."

"I'll do that later." She grabbed the plastic water bottle he'd given her in the car and slid open his trash receptacle.

He jerked forward. "You don't need to do that. I recycle. I have a bin in the back."

Could the guy be any more perfect?

"Admirable, but you forgot this one." She plucked his beer bottle out of the trash and set it on the counter next to the water bottle.

"Oh, thanks. Everything's locked up for the night, so I'll be in my bedroom if you need anything else."

She could think of quite a few things she'd want from Rob, but none was appropriate for a crash survivor who didn't even know her own identity. She squeezed past him out of the kitchen. "Thanks."

When she made it to the bathroom, she stripped off her clothes and dropped them to the floor. Facing the mirror naked, she studied her body for any more tattoos or identifying marks.

She discovered tan lines from a bikini, and a few more bumps and scratches from the crash. Her toes sported purplish polish, and although no such color tipped her fingernails, they looked neat. So, she probably wasn't a homeless person.

She skimmed her hands over her forearms and wrists—no needle tracks.

She twisted around to try to get a look at the Rosalinda tattoo. She caught the tail end of a flourish with a rose. She'd have to get ahold of a hand mirror to see it completely.

She cranked on the water and stepped into the warm spray, wincing as it hit her sore body. Did she want to reclaim the identity of a person who had people out to kill her?

Those guys believed she'd died in the crash, or at least the fire. She'd be safe as long as they maintained that belief.

She couldn't have Rob or anyone else plastering her picture anywhere or looking into any missing persons reports—not yet, anyway. She needed more information before she could step back into what was obviously a dangerous existence.

She might just hang out in Paradiso while she investigated. If Rob had friends here, she could get a job without ID. She had to support herself until her memory returned.

And if it never did?

She could forge a new identity. She could start life anew in Paradiso…with Rob Valdez as her first friend.

THE FOLLOWING MORNING, Rob plunged his hand into the pockets of Jane's pants. Empty. Why had she had a knife in her pocket? It must've been in her pocket, or she'd grabbed it when she escaped from the car. But why grab a knife and not a purse with your ID and money?

To protect herself against the violent ex?

He tossed the olive green pants into the washing machine and then shook out the torn T-shirt. He fingered the label that claimed its origin as Mexico. Lots of clothes were made in Mexico.

He dropped the shirt in the machine with the pants. That was all she had.

He added a few more clothes to the wash and strolled into the kitchen. He'd let Jane sleep and put on some coffee.

He had other reasons for letting her sleep in. He grabbed a plastic bag from a drawer and picked up the water bottle she'd drunk from last night, pinching the neck between two fingers. He dropped the bottle into the bag.

It might be a little late to check Jane's fingerprints, as she could've stabbed him in his sleep last night, but he deserved to know whom he had in his house. If she'd committed a crime anywhere, she'd be in the database. If not, he'd be back to square one—housing a woman who was lying about her identity.

If she had a violent ex-husband after her, he could understand her hesitance, but if she trusted him enough to stay here, she should be able to trust him with her real name.

He sealed the bag and stuffed it into his backpack. Pulling a chair up to his kitchen table, he dragged his laptop in front of him. When he launched a search engine, he entered *Rosalinda murder.*

He clicked on a few promising articles but, after fifteen minutes, gave up on finding a murder case involving a girl named Rosalinda. He'd need a last name, a city.

Jane would never give him that info. The only reason she'd told him about her friend was because he'd spotted that tattoo. He dragged a hand through his hair and hunched over the laptop.

Why did he care? She'd be gone this morning, and he'd chalk it up to a strange encounter—one of many in his life. He'd keep it to himself. He should've reported that crash and burned-out car, but he understood and sympathized with people who wanted to stay beneath the radar, especially women on the run from domestic violence.

As he heard the water run in the bathroom, he wiped out his search history and brought up his email. He pushed back from the table and stuck his head down the hallway.

He called out. "How are you doing this morning?"

She shouted over the running water. "I feel okay. I appreciate the water and ibuprofen you left on the nightstand. Are my clothes done?"

He edged closer to the bathroom door and placed a hand against it. "Not yet. Wash is almost done, and then I'll put them in the dryer. I'll get some breakfast together."

Without waiting for a reply, he returned to the kitchen and broke some eggs in a bowl. He mixed them with some milk, dashed some pepper in there and dumped them into a frying pan sizzling with butter.

"Smells good." Jane wedged her hip against the counter, tugging at the hem of his T-shirt, which—even though it hit her midthigh—had never looked so good.

"Just some scrambled eggs and coffee." He stirred the eggs. "Toast?"

"I can do the toast." She took two steps into the kitchen, and he immediately felt her presence engulf him.

For a petite woman, she had an overwhelming presence. At least for him.

Still prodding the eggs in the pan, he reached across the counter, flipped up the lid on the bread box and grabbed a loaf of wheat. "You can use this. Do you take cream or sugar with your coffee? I don't have cream, but you can dump some milk in there."

"Black."

He tapped the spatula on the edge of the pan. "You can help yourself to the coffee."

She reached around him and poured out two cups of steaming, fragrant java.

He scooped the eggs onto plates and carried them from the kitchen, relieved to escape the close quarters with Jane. As he put the plates on the table, the buzzer from the washing machine went off. "That's your laundry. You can start eating without me, if you want."

He strode into the laundry room and transferred the clothes from the wash to the dryer. When he returned to the kitchen, she'd placed silverware, napkins and their coffee on the table.

"The toast just popped up. Butter and jam or just butter?"

"Just butter for me. I don't even know if I have jam."

She brought the toast to the table, as he sipped his coffee.

"Why are you waiting on me? You're the accident victim." He took the plate of toast from her and pulled out a chair. "Sit."

She touched her bandaged head. "I feel fine, except that my head throbs when the ibuprofen wears off."

"You might need stitches." He held up a hand. "You should see your doctor when you get home."

"Maybe I don't want to go home." She crunched into her toast, and a shower of crumbs fell onto her plate.

"You can't hide from him forever."

"Really?" She speared a clump of eggs on her plate. "Do you think you could find me a job in Paradiso?"

"A job." He sputtered up his coffee. "Here?"

"Seems like a good place to lie low for a while. Maybe you know someone who could, you know, hire me off the books for a bit just so I could make a little money."

The thought of Jane staying in Paradiso sent a cascade of emotions tumbling through his system, but the ones that affected his body got the jump on the ones that affected his mind, and he blurted out, "Yeah, I do."

"You do?" She scooted up in her seat, wrapping her hand around her coffee cup. "Who? Where?"

"It's nothing fancy, but the woman who makes the soup you had last night runs a small café in the middle of town and her niece is heading back to college and can't help her out anymore." Why was he dragging Rosie into this? "Do you have any experience in food service?"

"I do. I worked in fast food in high school and did some bartending in college." Her light brown eyes widened for a second, and then she rushed on. "I'd be happy to help your friend out with her business, and if she needs to get rid of me when her niece comes back, no problem."

"We'll go see her today." Rob shoved some toast in his mouth to keep himself from offering her anything else. At least if she stayed, he'd have some time to find out her real story.

As if to avoid questions, Jane kept the conversation through breakfast light and superficial.

After wolfing down most of her food, she waved a fork at him. "You're not in uniform. Do you have to work today?"

"Not until later." He eyed her hair tousled around the bandage and a small bruise high on her cheekbone. "Are you sure you don't need medical attention?"

"Why?" She clicked her coffee mug onto the table. "Do I look like I do?"

"You look…" He was going to say she looked even more appealing than she had last night, but his big mouth had already gotten him into enough trouble. "You look amazingly well after walking away from that accident and spending the day in the desert."

She patted her head. "I feel fine and so grateful to have gotten away from…my ex."

The buzzer from the dryer in the laundry room saved him from analyzing why she paused before mentioning her ex-husband—but he'd come back to that.

He jumped up from the table. "Your clothes are done. You can take a shower, and I'll take you to Rosie's."

"She's the woman with the café?"

"That's right."

"Thank you so much." Jane rubbed her nose with the back of her hand. "I'm glad you stopped."

"I don't know what you thought you were going to do out there at night by yourself with just a knife."

"I—I must've been stunned, disoriented." She sipped her coffee and her eyes met his over the rim. "Where is that knife?"

His heart stuttered in his chest. He had no intention of arming his strange guest. Of course, she could've grabbed a kitchen knife at any time last night and stabbed him through the heart—if she'd wanted to.

He jerked his thumb over his shoulder. "I think I left it in my truck. Why'd you have it?"

"Excuse me?" She folded her hands on the table like an innocent schoolgirl.

She always answered a question with a question to buy time. He didn't need the academy to teach him that—he'd lived it with his *familia*.

"The knife. Why did you grab a knife, of all things, when you escaped from the burning car? Why not grab your purse? Your phone?"

"I didn't grab the knife. It was in my pocket." She slurped the dregs of her coffee. "Protection."

Man, she was good.

"You don't need protection here."

Her jaw hardened. "I appreciate that, but I'd still like my knife back… Sentimental value."

"Sure." He raised his hands as if in surrender. "I didn't mean I was keeping it forever. You can get it when we go out to the truck."

"I can wait. I don't need it now." She laughed, which snapped the wire of tension stretched between them. "Point me to the laundry room, and I'll get my clothes."

"Through the kitchen." He leveled a finger at the slatted door between the kitchen and the laundry room.

She gathered the plates on the table, including his, and placed them in the sink on her way to the laundry. "Thanks for the breakfast."

Several seconds later, she emerged, clutching her pants and T-shirt to her chest. "The sooner I shower and dress, the faster I can get out of your hair."

"Happy to help."

Nodding, she sidled out of the kitchen and turned the corner to the hallway.

When he heard the door snap close and the water start, Rob let out a long breath. He didn't know what to make of Jane. Should he be foisting her onto Rosie?

He'd let Rosie make the determination. He had faith in her ability to judge someone's character—at least more faith than in his at the moment. Being near Jane scrambled his senses for some reason.

Less than fifteen minutes later, Jane emerged from the bathroom. Her wet hair lay in tangled waves over her shoulders.

Rob jumped up from his laptop. "I'm sorry. I should've put out a comb and some hair products for you."

She shrugged. "You can be excused. You're a bachelor...aren't you?"

"Look at this place." He swept his arm to the side, taking in the neat room, every pillow and book in place, and his face warmed as Jane cocked her head.

"Doesn't look like any bachelor pad I've ever seen."

"I'm kind of a neat freak, but you won't find many feminine touches or niceties in here." He marched past her. "However, I do have sisters, and they usually need an army of products and a ton of time to make themselves presentable."

She tugged on the ends of her wet locks. "Not very presentable, huh?"

He glanced over his shoulder, his face heating up even more. "I didn't mean that. You look amazing for being in that car accident yesterday. How's your head?"

"I think it looks better without the bandage—less severe, and I can cover it with my hair. It feels fine."

She wouldn't tell him if it didn't. He swept into his bathroom and grabbed some hair products and other toiletries. He carried out an armful and dumped them on the vanity of the guest bathroom.

When he turned, he almost plowed into Jane standing in the doorway. "Help yourself."

"Thanks. I'll see if I can look more…presentable."

She came out the second time, bunching the ends of her hair into her fists. "I guess I'll leave it curly."

"Looks fine. Can't even see the wound on your head."

"That's crazy that such a small cut could cause so much…blood."

"Head wounds bleed." He closed up his laptop. "Are you ready?"

She tucked the ripped hem of her shirt into her pants. "I am now. I hope your friend Rosie isn't picky."

He hoped Rosie didn't think he was crazy. They walked out to the Border Patrol truck, his own truck parked on the street in front of his house. He opened the door for her and helped her in with a guiding hand on her back, which stiffened at his touch.

If her ex had abused her, he could understand her jitters, but that still remained an *if* in his mind. A lot of her story didn't add up.

He scooted behind the wheel and she said, "My knife?"

Yeah, a lot of things didn't add up.

Reaching beneath the seat, he said, "I think I stashed it here."

His fingers traced the edge of the knife's handle, and he pushed it farther under the seat. "It's not here. I'll have a more thorough look later. Is that okay?"

She snapped her seat belt and gripped the strap with two hands. "Yeah, sure."

On the ride to Rosita's, Jane peppered him with questions about the town. When she'd gotten her fill, she slumped in her seat. "You know a lot for being relatively new here."

"I made it my business to find out everything

I could about Paradiso. I probably know more than some natives. You know how that goes."

She nodded. "I do."

He slid a gaze in her direction and then pointed out the windshield. "That's it."

"Cute."

He pulled in front of the café, and before he could get Jane's door, she'd hopped out and stood in front of the restaurant with her hands on her hips.

"Looks closed."

"She opens for lunch, but I know she's here." He raised an eyebrow. "Chickening out?"

"It's a restaurant, not a roller coaster." She charged past him and yanked open the front door.

He followed her into the cool confines of the tile-floored café with framed photos of Pancho Villa on the walls.

He called out, "Rosie? It's Rob Valdez. Are you here?"

The grandmotherly woman bustled from the back, patting the long braid, streaked with gray, that wrapped around her head. "Rob, it's too early for *desayuna*."

"I'm not here to eat, Rosie." He nodded toward Jane, twisting her fingers in front of her. "I have a…friend, Jane, who's looking for a job—short term. She's in a little trouble, Rosie."

Rosie's warm brown eyes turned to Jane, assessing her from head to toe. Her face broke into a smile. "*Sí, sí. Puedo ayudar.* I can help. Have you had some experience, *mija*?"

Jane smiled back, the expression lighting up her face. Then she broke into fluent Spanish that put his to shame.

Chapter Four

Her lips were moving faster than her brain and her brain was freaking out, but when Rosie responded to her in Spanish, Jane kept the smile plastered to her face.

How did she know Spanish so well? The mirror had shown her paler skin than Rob's, but that didn't mean anything. She could be half-Latina. The Rosalinda tattooed on her back? Maybe that *was* her name, a family name.

She held up one hand and said in English, "I'm a little rusty. Do you mind continuing in English?"

Rosie chuckled and nudged Rob with her elbow. "She's being polite, Rob. Her Spanish is better than yours."

Rob's eyes narrowed as they assessed her. "It is, isn't it?"

Jane swallowed and turned to Rosie. "I do have another favor to ask of you. As I explained to you, I had to leave my situation quickly and

I'm trying to keep a low profile. That means I don't have any of my credit cards or any cash. Would you be willing to pay me in advance so that I can get a motel room and maybe a few things to wear?"

Rosie's bright eyes flicked from her to Rob. "I thought you and Rob…"

Rob cut off Rosie with a sharp cough. "Jane *is* my friend. Of course, you're staying with me, Jane. I thought I made myself clear."

"Rob is a very good man—the best." Rosie folded her hands and held them beneath her chin. "I know he will help you."

Rob smacked his hand on the countertop, probably wondering how he'd gotten in so deep. "I have a few things to do before I report to the station, so I'll leave you ladies to get ready for the lunch crowd. Thanks, Rosie. Good luck, Jane."

When the door closed behind Rob, Rosie asked, "Are you a friend of Rob's from LA?"

Los Angeles? That was big and sprawling enough to cover all situations.

"Yes, we're friends from LA."

Rosie shook her head. "Such a sad situation for him, but he's a strong man."

"He is." Jane bit her bottom lip. Had his wife left him? Was he in witness protection? Did his dog die?

"I'm glad you're here, Jane." Rosie brushed her hands together. "I'll explain what I need, and you can let me know if you have any questions."

For the next few hours, Jane wiped down tables and plastic menus, refilled the condiments at each station, prepped little plastic baskets for chips by dropping a sheet of paper in each one and stacking them, and even helped out Sal the cook in the kitchen.

Her head still throbbed a little and her memories were as elusive as ever, but this job had given her a purpose for now and that was what she needed—along with money, clothes, an ID. At least she had a place to stay.

She wouldn't hold Rob to that promise made for Rosie's benefit. Maybe the advance Rosie gave her would be enough to get into a motel.

She knew she couldn't stay in this town forever, pretending to be someone she wasn't, someone without an identity, someone without a home or family. But the thought of delving into her past frightened her. She'd be walking right into a murderous plot.

Paradiso could be her jumping-off point, a place from which to launch an investigation of her identity. And maybe Rob Valdez could help her.

"Two minutes until opening." Rosie stood in the middle of the floor, hands on her ample hips. *"Estás lista?"*

"I'm ready." Jane used the corner of a white towel to rub an imaginary spot on one of the tabletops. "Let 'em in."

Rosie unlocked the door and flipped the sign to Open. "It's a slow stream at first, but then we get the employees from the pecan processing plant and there's a rush."

"Bring 'em on, Rosie."

Jane handled her first few tables as if she'd been born to it. Maybe she was a waitress—with people out to kill her.

The lunch rush had her hopping, and she reconsidered the notion that she'd been a waitress in her previous life as she forgot items and spilled iced tea all over.

Rosita's did a brisk take-out business, and a line of customers had formed at the counter to pick up their orders.

Jane's gaze flicked over the line of people, and when a man yelled out that he wanted extra chips with his order, her blood ran cold in her veins. That voice.

With trembling hands, she delivered the salsa to her table and scurried back to the kitchen, keeping her head down. She pressed a hand against the butterflies in her belly as she leaned against the food prep counter.

The man who'd yelled out for food sounded like one of the guys who'd set her car on fire.

Why would he still be in this town? She wiped her sweaty palms on the pants covering her thighs. She'd imagined it. What had she really heard of that man's voice?

She ducked her head to peer through the window from the kitchen to the dining room. She hadn't seen the men at the scene of the accident and couldn't identify them, which put her at a distinct disadvantage. She remembered the black boots with the silver tips, but any number of people could be wearing those.

"Taking a break?" Anna, the other waitress, backed into the kitchen, her hands clutching two empty plates. "It can get hectic. If you need a breather from the dining room, you can package some of these to-go orders."

"I-if that's okay." Jane surveyed the containers of food crowding the countertop. Even if the voice didn't belong to one of the men from the highway, it had rattled her. She didn't want to serve food looking over her shoulder.

"More than okay." Anna picked up a slip of paper on top of one of the containers and waved it in the air. "Here are the orders. Just bag them and staple the slips to the handles of the plastic bags. Rosie will grab them and call them out by number."

"Got it."

For the remaining fifteen minutes of the

lunch rush, Jane packaged the orders and kept her head down. She'd been mistaken. There would be no reason for those men to be in Paradiso. They thought she was dead, incinerated in that car. They'd be reporting back to whoever wanted her dead. Husband? Boyfriend?

She shivered and then jumped when someone patted her on the shoulder.

Rosie's pat turned into a squeeze. "I'm sorry I scared you, *mija.* I just wanted to let you know you did a good job today. I'm glad Rob brought you to me, and now he's here for lunch. Go see."

A lock of hair had escaped from Jane's ponytail, and she tucked it behind her ear as she sidled past Rosie out of the kitchen.

Seated at a table by the window, Rob raised his hand. Her heart skipped a beat when she saw him, which she put down to the fact that his was the only familiar face she had in her sparse memory bank.

On her way to his table, she touched Anna's arm. "Do you need help with the tables?"

"Jose will clean those. Go have lunch and leave. You did all the setup today, so I'll take care of closeout."

Lunch? Was that what Rob was doing here? He wanted lunch with her. This morning it seemed he couldn't wait to wash his hands of her. That was before Rosie corralled him into taking her in.

As she approached Rob's table, he jumped from his seat and held out her chair. She smiled her thanks.

Rob had already proved his trustworthiness. He hadn't run to the cops, even though he was part of law enforcement himself. She should tell him about her predicament. She needed an ally.

Anna had already delivered a basket of chips, a bowl of salsa and a couple of glasses of water to Rob's table. Jane looked at the chips and wrinkled her nose.

"Hazards of the job. You're sick of chips and salsa already." Rob grabbed a chip and dunked it into the salsa. "If you haven't tried Rosie's salsa yet, you're missing out. It's the best north of the border…and maybe even south."

Jane took his advice and scooped up a healthy dose of salsa with a sturdy chip and bit off the corner. The heat of the jalapeño made her eyes water, but just a little.

She sniffed and said, "It's good."

"How did your first day of work go?"

"Rosie is so sweet and Anna, Sal, Jose—all of them." She flicked at the corner of the plastic menu in front of her. Could she keep working here if her tormentors had stayed in the area? Where would she go if she didn't?

Rob briefly touched her hand and then snatched it back. “Is everything okay? How are you feeling? How’s your head?”

She stroked the hair on the side of her head, covering the gash in her skull where her memories had leaked out. “It throbs now and then, but it’s not giving me any trouble.”

“I still think you need to see a doctor, sooner rather than later.”

Jane nudged his foot with hers as Anna came up to the table. “Ready to order?”

“You know me, Anna. Same old, same old.”

Anna tapped her head. “Burrito with carnitas, wet with green. How about you, Jane?”

“I’ve been eyeing those chicken tacos all day.”

“Good choice. Drinks?”

They both ordered iced teas, and then Rob planted his elbows on the table. “Tell me what happened.”

Jane blinked. “What happened? At work?”

He swept his hand across the surface of the table. “You had an abusive ex, you left him and he came after you. Did he cause the car accident? Are you going to report him?”

She licked her lips and took a sip of water. “It may be worse than that.”

Folding his arms, Rob hunched forward across the table, his dark eyes burning into her. “You can tell me.”

Could she? How did she even begin to tell him of her predicament? He'd probably want to take her straight to the hospital. Straight to the police. She couldn't allow that. For some reason, she couldn't allow that.

She rubbed her arms and opened her mouth to speak, but Anna interrupted with their iced tea. "Food will be up in a minute. More salsa?"

"Please." Rob tapped his glass. "And more water when you get the chance, Anna."

Anna spun around to get Rob's water, and he dumped a packet of sugar into his tea. "What were you going to say?"

"Before I get to that, can I ask you a question?"

"I'm an open book."

"I can second that." Anna returned with their food and topped off Rob's water. "This guy can't keep his mouth shut."

"Is it your job to eavesdrop now?" He picked up his fork and waved it at Anna's back. "You're setting a bad example for Jane."

Jane poked at her taco. If Rob were a talker, would he be able to keep her secrets?

He stabbed a piece of burrito and swept it through the salsa verde on his plate. "What's your question?"

"Why'd you agree to help me? I figured as

a law enforcement officer, you'd feel bound to call the police."

He shrugged. "You were in a single-car crash. You didn't destroy any property or hurt anyone but yourself."

She stirred her tea with a straw, and the ice tinkled against the side of the glass. "It's more than that, isn't it?"

Rob sucked up half his tea through the straw before replying. "It was the abusive ex that got me. My mother had an abusive husband."

"Your father?"

"No." The line of Rob's jaw hardened, and he plunged his fork into his burrito. "My stepfather. My dad died not too long after I was born."

"I'm sorry." She picked up her taco and tapped the edge of the hard shell against her plate. "And then your mother married a man who abused her."

"Yeah, and I was too young to do anything about it. I'm the youngest of five." He'd placed the tines of his fork on the edge of his plate, and his hand curled into a fist on the table.

"Is that why you went into law enforcement, to correct all the wrongs you couldn't set right as a kid?"

His head jerked up, and he took a gulp of water. "Maybe. Are you a psychoanalyst or something?"

Was she?

"N-no. And your other siblings? Did they go into the law, too?"

He snorted. "The other side of the law. I have two brothers and two sisters. One of my brothers is in prison. The other is an ex-con, an OG who still holds court in East LA."

"Wow. And your sisters? I'm afraid to ask." She took a bite of her food, her teeth crunching into the taco. She'd been trying to buy time, not realizing she'd get Rob's dramatic life story.

"My oldest sister is married to a criminal, repeating my mother's sad story, and my other sister is getting her doctorate at the University of Texas in Austin."

"How did you and your sister escape the family legacy?"

"Sheer willpower and a little luck."

She handed him his fork. "I didn't mean to ruin your appetite."

"Yeah, it's not exactly my favorite lunchtime topic." He attacked his food again.

Rob's attention to his lunch gave her some time to think of how she was going to frame her story. What was to frame? She lost her memory in the crash, and those two men gave her reason to believe she was in danger. Rob could help her.

She finished her food, took a sip of tea and

patted her mouth with her napkin. As she took a deep breath, Rob's phone rang.

He glanced at it and held up one finger. "Excuse me. I gotta take this. It's work."

He tapped the phone. "Valdez."

He listened for a second, a crease forming between his eyebrows. "Yeah, yeah. You think it's El Gringo Viejo?"

Jane's heart slammed against her chest. El Gringo Viejo? Where had she heard that before? As she gripped the edge of the table with her hands, the voice of one of the men from the crash site came back to her and a piercing pain lanced the side of her head.

El Gringo Viejo was the person who wanted her dead.

Chapter Five

Rob half listened to his coworker as Jane's face turned white. He raised his eyebrows and pushed a glass of water toward her. Damn, she needed a doctor.

The voice on the phone repeated, "How many tunnels are left to check, Rob?"

"Maybe three. Hey, can we continue this when I get back to the station? I'm in the middle of something."

He ended the call with the other agent and grabbed Jane's hand. "Are you okay? You look like you're about to pass out or be sick or both."

"Just got a little woozy. I'm okay."

No matter how many times Jane said that to him, he didn't believe her. Who crawled from an accident like that with a head injury, on the run from some violent ex-husband, and refused to go to the police or the hospital? Refused to even call family or go home?

"Have some water."

Jane—whose last name must remain a mystery—had more secrets than a Vegas magician. But she was no criminal, at least not that he'd discovered, yet.

He'd run her prints and nothing had come back. That didn't mean a whole helluva lot. She could be a lucky criminal who'd never been caught. At least she hadn't tried to jack Rosita's.

Jane came up for air after chugging a glass of water, a little more color in her cheeks. "Do you mind if I take a nap at your place while you're at work? I think I just need some sleep."

A stranger in his house alone? A stranger swimming in secrets, steeped in lies? He'd offered. Did he think she'd be there only the same time as he would?

"Oh, oh." She covered her mouth with one hand. "You were just pretending before with Rosie, weren't you? I'm sorry. Of course you're not going to allow some random person to stay in your house while you're gone."

Heat suffused his chest and Rob took a deep breath, battling to keep it from washing into his face. He'd offered his home to her, and she'd taken him at his word. And he'd meant it…at the time. His fellow agents were always warning him that even though Paradiso was light-years from LA in danger, he shouldn't treat the place like a friendly little town.

They were too close to the border for that. Hadn't Las Moscas, the most active cartel in their area, left a couple of severed heads on a Border Patrol agent's doorstep?

Didn't stop him from feeling like a jerk.

"Look..." He held out his hand.

Shaking her head, she ignored the gesture. "No, really. I understand completely."

"Let me finish." He pushed away his plate. "I'll get you a room for the afternoon so you can sleep and rest up. Then you can come over for dinner, and we'll play it by ear. I'm not sure you should be alone anyway, whether at my place or at a motel."

This time, she put out her hand for a shake. "I accept your kind offer. I can pay you back for the room once I get some wages from Rosie."

He clasped her hand, feeling it tremble slightly in his. "Don't worry about paying me back."

"Sorry to interrupt." Rosie appeared next to their table, clutching a wad of bills. "This is for you, Jane, for your work today. I pay you in cash. You can come tomorrow, too, same time?"

"Absolutely." Jane jumped from her chair and hugged Rosie. "Thank you so much."

Rosie tapped her finger against the bruise beneath Jane's eye. "You take care of yourself, and I'll see you tomorrow. Do you need clothes?"

"I'll pick up a few things." Jane held up the money Rosie had just given her.

"I have that covered, Rosie."

Rosie winked. "You're a good boy, *mijo*."

As Rosie disappeared into the kitchen, Jane's smile faded from her face. "Was that offer for Rosie's benefit, too?"

Rob swallowed hard. "No. You look about the same size as my buddy's wife. I was going to ask her for a few things—I swear."

"I'm just kidding around." Jane pressed a hand against her heart. "I do understand why you wouldn't want a stranger in your house when you're not there. This all could be an elaborate ruse, and I might have an accomplice waiting outside town with a truck, ready to clean you out."

Rob tugged on his earlobe. "Wow. I didn't even think of that one."

"We'd better get going if I'm checking into a motel." Jane shoved away from the table and collected their dirty dishes. She carried them to the kitchen and said goodbye to the staff.

Rob waved on the way out of the restaurant. As he helped Jane into his truck, he said, "We'll make a quick stop at the store for a few things."

The few things turned into a basket filled with ibuprofen, vitamins, bottled water, juice, a couple of T-shirts, snacks and other things to assuage his guilt.

He booked her into the Paradiso Motel and stashed her new belongings, her only belongings, in the room. He snapped the key cards on the credenza next to the TV.

"Should I take one of those, just in case?"

Her whiskey-colored eyes widened. "In case I pass out or die in the room?"

Fear tingled at the back of his neck, and he clapped his hand over it. "Don't say that. Just in case you need some help. Do you mind?

"I mean, I'm just as much a stranger to you as you are to me. You probably shouldn't give your motel key to a strange man."

"Strange man? I spent the night in your house last night, and you got me a job today." Her lush lips twisted. "I feel like I've known you all my life."

He grunted. "You're very funny."

"Take the key." She wedged a hand on her hip. "I'm going to ask for something in return, though."

"The knife."

"Read my mind. If I'm going to be alone in this room with an extra key floating around out there, I'd prefer to have a little protection." She widened her stance, as if digging her heels into the carpet. "I know it's in your truck, Rob."

"You're probably right." He grabbed a bottle of water from the minifridge. "Wait here and I'll get it for you."

The door to her room slammed behind him as he stepped outside. He'd get her the knife for kicking her out of his house. She must think her ex, or whoever, was headed this way.

He chewed on his bottom lip. She'd been about to open up to him over lunch, but they'd gotten off track. What had she said? The truth was probably worse than a violent, vindictive ex?

He ducked into his truck and felt under the driver's seat. His fingers wrapped around the knife and he pulled it out.

Cupping it in his hand, he examined the intricate metalwork in silver. The knife had been crafted in Mexico, like her clothing. Like her Spanish?

He'd get to the bottom of things tonight.

ROB SPENT MOST of the rest of the afternoon at the station doing follow-up work on the cartel's tunnels under the border. The Border Patrol had hit the mother lode when one of the agents, Clay Archer, had come into possession of a map detailing the tunnels Las Moscas had painstakingly created for their drug trade.

As Rob stretched at his desk and thought

about Jane back at the motel, Clay plopped down behind his own desk and fired a pen at him. "Daydreaming, Valdez?"

"Yeah, daydreaming about getting out of here." Rob rolled the pen toward him with the toe of his boot and bent over to pick it up. Keeping his head beneath the desk, Rob asked, "Is April home right now? I have a favor to ask her."

"She's home. Do you want me to pass it along to her?"

Rob popped up from beneath the desk, holding the pen between two fingers. "I'll just drop by and see her. I know you're working late, and my request doesn't have anything to do with you."

"Mysterious." Clay held up a finger as the phone on his desk rang.

As Clay flipped through a file, Rob grabbed the opportunity to get out before Clay started asking probing questions. He shoved his laptop and some files into his shoulder bag and, on his way out the door, held up his hand at Clay still on the phone.

April would tell her husband everything, anyway. After the start those two had, they kept no secrets between them. But Rob didn't have to give Clay a head start on the ribbing.

He drove out to Clay and April's place and parked on the street in front. As promised, April was home. Her work as an accountant allowed her to work from the house.

Clay must've given her a heads-up because she came out to the porch to wait for him as he approached the front door.

She gave him a hug. "Clay told me you were on the way with a mysterious favor to ask."

"Clay's paranoid. It's not all that mysterious." He took off his hat as he stepped over the threshold, and their dog immediately bounded at him. He scratched Denali behind the ear. "Hey, boy."

"What do you need?" She picked up a glass of lemonade from the coffee table where she'd been working and raised it. "Can I get you something to drink? It's still hot as blazes and I heard we have a monsoon on the way."

"Yeah, the wettest winter I ever spent was a summer in Tucson, or something like that." He shook his head. "I don't need anything but your clothes."

April grabbed the hem of her T-shirt and wiggled her hips. "Ooh, no wonder you didn't tell my husband."

Rob laughed. "Not those clothes. I have a friend who's in kind of a…situation, and she needs some clothes—nothing fancy, just a few pairs of shorts, a couple of T-shirts, maybe some jeans. She's about your size, maybe shorter, so

I thought you might have something she could borrow."

April tilted her head and wrapped a lock of blond hair around one finger. "I have some stuff. Is this a *particular* friend?"

He kind of knew he wasn't going to escape April's matchmaking efforts. The woman had a caretaking streak a mile long and figured everyone needed to be as happy as she and Clay were.

"No, just a friend in need."

"Well, you know those are my favorite kind." She crooked a finger at him. "This way, Agent Valdez. I'll throw a few things together for your…friend."

Thirty minutes later, Rob staggered from the house, bags hanging from his fingertips that included enough clothes to outfit a sorority. With a wave out the window of his truck, he pulled away from the curb and made his way back to town.

He might as well pick up some dinner before he collected Jane from the motel. She could go through April's clothes at his place.

As he rolled up to the stop sign to turn onto the main street, his foot hit the brake hard and his truck lurched. He squinted through his sunglasses and watched as Jane tripped down the steps of the library.

What happened to her nap? Had she decided

to get a Pima County library card while she hid out from her ex?

A car rattled past her, and she jumped, craning her head over her shoulder. She continued to glance behind her as she made her way down the street, never noticing him.

A breath hitched in his throat, as a man wearing a baseball cap and walking toward her seemed to slow his gait and flash her some kind of sign with his hand. Jane's step never even faltered, and Rob eased out a sigh.

He waited until she turned the corner, most likely on her way back to the motel, but even that seemed doubtful now. He wheeled onto the library's side street and scrambled out of the truck. He poked his head around the edge of the building to make sure Jane wasn't making a repeat appearance, and then strode to the entrance.

He eyed the three computers available for public use. A senior citizen was parked at one, playing a game of solitaire. The other two monitors glared at him.

She had to have been here using the computers. What else? She didn't walk out with any books under her arm. Standing between the two machines, he tapped the keyboards—one with each hand.

Password screens popped up, and the old man seated at the other computer pointed to a slip of paper attached to the top of the monitor, his crooked finger waving in the air. “Passwords are right there.”

“Thank you, sir.” Rob pulled one keyboard toward him and entered the password. The monitor woke up and displayed a desktop with several available applications.

Rob ran the mouse across the application icons, hovering over a web browser. “Did you see a woman using one of these computers while you were here? She just left.”

The man removed his glasses, and his faded blue eyes assessed Rob from head to toe. He leaned forward and cupped his mouth with his hand. “Official business?”

“Yes, yes, it is. Official business.” Rob cleared his throat.

“She was here.” The old man raised his eyes to the ceiling. “Pretty little thing with hair the color of caramel candy.”

Rob’s hand jerked. He supposed Jane did have hair the color of caramel. “That’s her. Which computer was she using and…uh, did you notice what she was doing?”

“She was using the one on the end, but I could still smell her.” The man’s prominent nose twitched with the memory.

Rob raised one eyebrow. “Her smell?”

“Lemons—fresh and tart—just like my Lois.”

The man closed his eyes, lost in the memory of his Lois.

Rob coughed as he sidled in front of the computer Jane had been using. "Did you notice what she was doing?"

The man opened one eye. "Surfing the internet. Why don't you ask Julie, if this is official business? She can log you in to the young woman's session."

"I was just going to do that." Rob squared his shoulders and marched to the reference desk. The old guy obviously knew more about how the public computers worked than he did.

Julie looked up at his approach. "Hi, Rob. Do you need something?"

"A woman was in here using one of the computers, and I'd like to find out what she looked up."

"I can do that." Julie came from behind the reference desk and patted his arm. "All work and no play."

Rob ducked his head. Julie had a daughter somewhere in Phoenix she wanted him to meet, but he hated setups and he hated blind dates. "We're always busy."

Julie dropped her voice to a whisper. "Is this woman a drug dealer? A mule?"

"Nothing that serious." He put his finger to his lips and jerked his thumb at the man still playing solitaire.

Julie laid a hand on the man's shoulder. "Beating your own records, Frank?"

"I'm workin' on it, Julie."

Julie perched on the chair in front of the computer Jane had vacated recently and tapped on the keyboard. She logged out and then logged back in. A few clicks later and she pushed back from the table.

"There you go. We're back in her session. You can look at her browsing history to see what she's been up to." Julie traced the tip of her finger across the seam of her closed mouth. "And I won't tell a soul."

"Thanks, Julie."

"Anytime you get a break, I'll give you my daughter's cell phone number."

"I'll remember that." Julie's poor daughter would probably be mortified to discover her mother was playing matchmaker for her.

Rob scooted closer to the monitor and brought up the history of Jane's browsing session.

As he scrolled through the searches on drugs and drug cartels, his heart began to pound in his chest. When he got to the bottom and read the first search she'd entered, the blood pounded in his temples.

Jane had been searching for information on El Gringo Viejo—one of the most notorious drug suppliers in Mexico.

Chapter Six

The knock on the motel door made her jump. Wiping her sweaty palms on her pants, she stalked toward the door and leaned forward to peek through the peephole.

Rob took a step back so she could see his whole body. Several bags hung at his sides.

She puffed a breath from her lips, closed the knife and shoved it into her front pocket. She'd had a scare on the street earlier when a stranger wearing a cap had stared at her, and then flashed her a peace sign. She'd been afraid he'd followed her here.

She swung the door open and took a step back. "I thought maybe you weren't coming back to get me."

His eyebrows collided over his nose as he lifted his shoulders. "Why would you think that?"

"I don't know." She stood to the side and

gestured him into the room. "Out of sight, out of mind."

"You may have been out of sight but never out of my mind." He held up the bags, stuffed with clothing, swinging them from his fingers. "I even got you some stuff to wear."

She pressed a hand against her warm cheek. What did he mean she was never out of his mind? And the clothes? She shouldn't get too dependent on Rob, but what choice did she have? He was it—the extent of her relationships. She could probably add Rosie, Anna and the cooks and busboys at Rosita's to her list. And El Gringo Viejo.

Why did a drug dealer want to see her dead?

"Th-that's so thoughtful of you. I hope you didn't go to any trouble on my behalf." She lifted up one foot encased in a new sandal. "I was able to buy a few things at the thrift shop, too."

"Oh, you went out?" He turned the bags upside down over the bed and dumped out the articles of clothing. They landed on the bedspread in a tangle of colors and textures.

"Just for a short time." She sat on the edge of the mattress and picked through the items. "Where'd you get all this stuff? Looks all the same size and hardly thrift store quality."

"I hit up my coworker's wife. I figured you

two to be about the same size." He cocked his head, his gaze scanning her from head to toe. "Maybe she's a little taller. My other buddy's girlfriend is maybe more your size, but…"

"But what?"

"She's a cop. She's attending the police academy right now."

Jane curled her hands around the edge of a floral sundress, bunching the silky material in her fists. "Oh."

"Yeah, oh." He ran a hand through his thick dark hair. "She'd be suspicious…and you wouldn't want that, would you?"

"No. I mean, the fewer people who know about my particular situation, the better."

"Your situation." Rob dropped his chin to his chest. "Anyway, the woman who gave me the clothes, April, she's always trying to help someone—to a fault."

"Sounds like you."

"I told you. I'm a sucker for…ladies in distress."

The tension between them vibrated like a plucked string. She grabbed one of the T-shirts and held it up. "Nice. Thank you."

"What did you do today besides hit the thrift store?" He meandered to the window and flicked aside the drapes, peering outside.

"Slept mostly." She patted her stomach. "I

hope some dinner is in our future. I'm starving. I—I can pay half from the money Rosie gave me."

He dropped the curtain fold and pivoted toward her. "That doesn't make any sense. You need that money to get back on your feet, get yourself home or wherever it is you want to go. I already ordered us some dinner, and if we don't get going, the dinner is going to get to the house before we do."

"I'll try some of these things on at your place, then." She began to shovel the clothes back into the bags. "Tell your friend thanks for me."

"Will do." He waited for her with his back to the door, his arms folded.

Had April questioned him about her? Was he having second thoughts?

Maybe she should get out of Paradiso before El Gringo Viejo came looking for her. Hopefully the two men who'd set fire to her car had done a good job convincing their boss that they'd killed the prey.

She needed help—real help from a professional to get her memory back. She hadn't wanted to face her past, but now it seemed as if it were more dangerous not to remember.

She grabbed the bags full of clothes, patted the knife in her pocket and spun around with a smile pasted on her face. "I'm ready."

He opened the door and stood aside for her, saying, "I kept the room for you, so if you want to get settled here, you have a place."

She nodded, blinking her eyes. Something had changed. Rob didn't want her in his house, didn't want to help her anymore. He'd be even more reluctant to help her if he knew she had some connection to El Gringo Viejo.

When they got to his house, he pointed to the room she'd used the night before. "You're welcome to try on some of those clothes. I'm sure you're sick of what you're wearing now, although that T-shirt from Rosita's looks good on you."

She pulled the T-shirt away from her body, glancing down at the logo for the café. "Rosie saved my life today...and you. Thank you. Have I said thank you?"

"You pulled a knife on me, instead."

She clutched a bag of clothing to her chest. "I'm sorry for that. You can understand why I did it."

"Sure." His lips stretched into a fake smile.

"I'll try some of these on." She dragged her feet down the hallway to Rob's guest room. He was definitely having second thoughts. Maybe April, the owner of the clothes, told him he was crazy. Maybe he'd told the other friend, the cop, and she was on her way right now.

She slammed the door behind her and dropped the bag of clothes on the floor. She'd stay away from Rob and his friends. Work at Rosita's for some cash, keep the motel room and make her way to Tucson and find herself a psychiatrist. If she were mixed up with this El Gringo Viejo and the cartels, she could disappear. Get a new identity. What would it matter? She had no identity now.

She pulled on and yanked off jeans, capris, shorts, blouses, T-shirts, sweaters. April had covered all the bases.

She left on a pair of olive capris and a red T-shirt and surveyed the rainbow pile of clothes on the bed. She'd use the money Rosie gave her today to get settled, and she'd get out of Rob's way.

She swallowed the lump in her throat. Leaving Rob would be like losing her only friend.

Squaring her shoulders, she followed the smell of garlic into the kitchen. She tipped her nose in the air. "Italian?"

Rob glanced up from dumping some spaghetti onto a plate. "Is that okay?"

"Smells good." She popped a lid from a plastic container. "I'll do the salad."

Stepping back from his task, Rob waved a fork up and down her body. "The clothes fit?"

The look in his eyes sent a little tingle up her

thighs. He may have changed his mind about being friends with her, but the attraction he had for her hadn't died out.

Her fingers fidgeted with the hem of the T-shirt. "Most of them. She *is* taller than I am, but it's close enough. Beggars can't be choosers."

"Don't think of yourself as a beggar." He nabbed a drop of marinara sauce from the counter with his thumb and sucked it into his mouth. "You're someone in need, and April likes nothing more than helping someone in need."

"Did you tell her about me?" She pinched the edges of the salad bowls between her fingers.

"Just a few basics. She's not the one you have to worry about." He turned his back to her, and she nearly dropped the bowls.

"Worry about?" She set the dishes on the table harder than she'd intended and they sent a clacking sound through the air that made her grit her teeth.

"I mean about being nosy. April just has to hear someone needs her help and she's the first to offer a hand. Emily's the cop—or at least she's going through the police academy right now. She's the one who'd want your life story."

Jane scooped her hair back from her face and said, "It's a good thing she's busy with the academy, then."

She hovered over the salads, her face turned

away from him, waiting for a reply. All she got was the crinkling of foil.

"Do you like garlic bread?"

She supposed she did, as the smell of that bread had been making her mouth water ever since she'd left the bedroom. She took a deep breath. "I do."

He emerged from the kitchen, a plate of spaghetti and meatballs in each hand, a wedge of garlic bread balanced on the edge of the plates.

Rob tipped his head back. "Do you want to get some silverware? It's in the drawer by the toaster."

She ducked around him into the kitchen and pulled open the drawer. She grabbed two place settings and spun around, almost bumping into Rob, who'd already delivered the food to the table.

His eyes widened for a split second as his gaze dropped to the utensils clutched in her hands. "Knives for spaghetti?"

"Those meatballs looked pretty big. I'd prefer to cut mine with a knife civilly instead of trying to saw it with the edge of the fork and have it shoot across the table." Her lips turned up at the corners, but her grip on the silverware tightened. He didn't trust her with a knife in her hand.

Would he ever forget their meeting in the desert? What had he expected her to do when confronted with a stranger at night in the desert after someone had just tried to kill her?

Of course, Rob didn't know her whole story, and just as she'd been about to tell him, El Gringo Viejo had come between them. She couldn't tell him now. He'd never believe her.

"Good point." He scooted past her, his body tense. "I'll get some water. I'd offer you some wine, but I'm not sure your head needs alcohol right now—unless you want some."

"Water is fine." All she needed was to get drunk and babble her troubles into his sympathetic ears—ears that didn't seem so sympathetic now. Although maybe if she got loaded, her inhibitions would fall away and she might remember something of her life before the crash. She'd have to ask her psychiatrist if that would work—when she got one.

She positioned the silverware on either side of the plates in perfect order. How did she remember inconsequential stuff like place settings but not her own name? Another question for her future shrink.

She sat in front of one plate and waited until Rob returned with the glasses of water before plunging her fork into the steaming pasta. She twirled the spaghetti around the tines and sucked it off her fork. The red sauce dribbled on her chin and she dabbed it with a paper towel.

He pulled the salad bowl toward him and stabbed at a piece of lettuce. “How long do you plan to stay in Paradiso?”

“Until I feel safe.” That was no lie. How could she go out into the world with people trying to kill her? They thought she was dead. They wouldn’t be looking for her. Would they be watching the TV for news about a car wreck with a dead body burned to a crisp? And when they didn’t see it, would they go back?

“You don’t like the spaghetti?” Rob jabbed his fork in the air toward her plate.

“It’s good.” She picked up the knife and cut one of the huge meatballs in half and then quarters. “You see how neat that is?”

“I guess I’d better not stuff the whole thing in my mouth like I usually do.”

Prodding the other meatball on her plate with her fork, she shook her head. “You’re lying. I can’t imagine you doing that.”

“What would make you feel safe?”

She dropped her fork. Was he trying to catch her off guard?

“Oh, just to know my ex isn’t looking for me.” She toyed with the pasta. “Do you feel safe?”

Two could play this game.

His dark brows shot up. “From you?”

She picked up the knife and plunged it into a meatball. “Are you afraid I’m going to stab you in the night?”

“*Are* you?”

“I already slept under your roof one night—uneventfully. Besides, I didn’t mean feel safe from me. Do you feel safe from your past?”

The Adam’s apple in his neck bobbed as he swallowed—and he didn’t even have any food in his mouth.

“My past? I feel safe. I escaped it, remember?”

She tilted her head. “Did you?”

“What does that mean?” He gulped some water. “Are you sure you’re not a shrink? You talk like one.”

“How do you know what a shrink talks like?”

“Got me.” He formed his fingers into a gun and pointed at her. “Are you kidding? With my upbringing, the school was always sending me to the school psychologist. ‘Are you okay, Roberto?’ ‘How does that make you feel, Roberto?’”

He’d changed his voice with the questions to mimic a woman.

“How did it all make you feel? The violence? The instability?”

He pushed away his salad and attacked his spaghetti. “Made me feel like taking control of everything and never letting go. Made me feel like hunting down every drug dealer and giving him some rough justice."

His words caused goose bumps to ripple across her skin, but she resisted rubbing her arms. She took a sip of water. "So, you became a Border Patrol agent."

He nodded, sucking the last of his pasta into his mouth. The action resulted in a drop of marinara landing on his chin.

She crumpled the paper towel in her lap and raised it to dab his chin.

He flinched, but she swiped it off anyway.

"Can't take me anywhere." He scrubbed his own paper towel across his mouth until his chin was redder than the original drop of sauce.

"Do you feel like you make a difference in the drug war?"

"I wouldn't stay in this job if I didn't think that." He dragged the tines of his fork through the sauce on his plate. "And what about you? Where do you live? What do you do for a living? Do you have any children?"

She pinned her hands between her knees. She shouldn't have gotten personal with him. He demanded reciprocity. He'd shown her his, and now he expected her to show him hers.

"I—I'm a teacher—an art teacher." She pressed a hand against her heart. Something felt so real about that statement. Could it be the truth? Were her memories brimming at the edge of her consciousness, ready to overflow and make her whole?

He nodded, stuffing a meatball—just a piece of one—into his mouth. When he finished chewing and swallowing, he said, "That would explain what you're doing out here in the middle of the summer."

It *would* explain that. She obviously hadn't been going to or coming from a job. Had she been in Mexico? She hadn't noticed the license plates on the car before it went up in flames. If she had memorized the license number, maybe she would've been able to discover her identity. Had she left a purse in the car? ID? Money? Why hadn't she thought of all that before scrambling from that car?

"Are you all right?" Rob planted his elbows on the table on either side of his plate.

The words expressed concern, but his face didn't match. His dark eyes drilled into her, probing her vacant mind. If he could read it, more power to him.

"I'm fine. I'd rather not discuss my life." She pushed back from the table so abruptly the chair tipped over, and she saved it from falling.

She stacked her bowl onto the plate. "Can I get your dishes? Are you finished?"

Rob curled his fingers around her wrist, his light touch feeling more like a vise due to the intensity in his dark eyes.

Her pulse fluttered, as she leaned toward him, the magnetic draw of his gaze reeling her into his realm. This attraction between them couldn't be stopped, even though she hadn't a clue who she was. She could be married with four children, and not even that possibility could dampen the fire that kindled in her belly for this man.

Her eyes drifted closed. Her lips parted. Her breath caught in her throat.

But when she felt the warmth of his mouth inches from her own, the imminent kiss turned into harsh words.

"How the hell do you know El Gringo Viejo?"

Chapter Seven

Jane blinked her whiskey-colored eyes, and Rob clenched his back teeth, trying hard not to imagine whether or not her lips would taste like the color of her eyes. He could've satisfied his curiosity by indulging in a small nip before dropping his bombshell, but that just didn't seem right.

Realizing she was still poised for the kiss that hung suspended between them, Jane jerked back. Her gaze darted around the room as if looking for an escape. Then she took a deep breath, her chest rising and falling in the red T-shirt borrowed from April.

When her eyes found their way back to his face, they narrowed. Her nostrils flared, and she pulled back her shoulders. Ready for conflict.

"Why do you think I know El Gringo Viejo?"

Squeezing his eyes shut, Rob pinched the bridge of his nose. Did he think this was going to be easy? He scooted his chair out from beneath the table and clasped his hands on his knees. "I saw your search history on the library computer."

Her left eye twitched. "You were spying on me all this time?"

He'd been around criminals long enough to know they went with a swift offense when backed into a corner. "Did you think I'd let a strange woman into my home for an overnight stay without doing a little checking?"

"You didn't do any checking that first night." She thrust out her chin.

"You were injured, confused. I wasn't going to turn you away, but I did keep that knife from you and I retained your water bottle for fingerprints."

Her head snapped up, and she gripped the seat of the chair. "You ran my fingerprints? You know who I am?"

"You probably already know I didn't find a match." He tilted his head to the side, studying her face. "So, I know you're not an art teacher. Teachers' prints are on file."

Her shoulders slumped in disappointment. "You didn't find out my identity from running my prints, so you followed me around this afternoon and snooped into my activities at the library?"

"Snooped?" He rolled his eyes, smacking his hands on his thighs.

She flinched.

"You're giving me too much credit. I happened to see you walk away from the library when I went to the main drag to pick up some food for dinner. You told me you were going to nap this afternoon, so I got curious. That's when I discovered your first search was for El Gringo Viejo." He crossed his arms over his chest and leaned back in his chair, as if to give her plenty of room to hang herself. "Why?"

She sucked in her cheek before answering, formulating her lie. "If I knew who he was, like you claimed, why would I be searching him?"

He snorted. "You randomly did a search on El Gringo Viejo the first opportunity you had? If you didn't know him or know who he was, why would you do that?"

"But I had heard his name before." She held up her finger and then lowered it to point it at him. "You mentioned El Gringo Viejo on a phone call you took during lunch at the café."

"You heard that and immediately did a search for him?" His fingers bit into his biceps. "That makes no sense. Try again."

"It sounded fascinating." She hopped up from the chair and spun away from him. "I was curious."

Hugging herself, she walked away from him

and stopped by the window to peer through the glass.

"Jane."

She hunched her shoulders and leaned her forehead against the windowpane.

"Do you know what I'm thinking right now?" He couldn't explain to her exactly the thoughts crossing his mind because along with irritation with her lies and his suspicions, he had a strong desire to take her in his arms. He couldn't explain it to himself, so he sure as hell wasn't going to admit it to her.

She shifted to display her profile. The defiance had gone out of her chin. Her long lashes and parted, pouting lips suggested a vulnerability all out of proportion to a woman who was a liar and possibly connected to the cartels.

She'd been playing him since the moment she flashed her knife at him. A place to stay, a job, clothing, meals, sex… That hadn't happened, but if he hadn't uncovered her search history at the library, they might be tangled up in his sheets right this minute.

He cleared his throat and repeated the dangerous question, the one he hoped she couldn't guess in a million years. "Do you know what I'm thinking?"

She turned to face him, tucking her hands behind her back like a chastened schoolgirl.

"You probably think I'm connected to El Gringo Viejo, that I was on some kind of drug run that went bad, or that I double-crossed him and the drug cartels and they retaliated by running me off the road and torching my car. Or you think I'm still in their good graces and this—" she flapped her arms at her sides "—is some kind of setup, some sort of infiltration into the Border Patrol through my seduction of you."

He felt his eyes pop out of their sockets like some kind of cartoon character, so he closed them and rubbed them with his fists. She'd come up with more scenarios than he'd let creep into his brain. Had she been seducing him?

"Is that close?" A little smile played about her lips, but her eyes drooped in sadness and he felt that crazy urge to charge across the room and engulf her in a bear hug.

"Close enough." He shoved his hands in his pockets. "Which is it, or is it all of the above?"

She turned back toward the window and doodled on the glass with her fingertip. "I don't know."

Rob blew out the breath he'd been holding, uttering a curse at the same time. "You're gonna have to tell me, or I'll have to…take action."

He crossed the room in a few long strides and touched her shoulder. "Just tell me, Jane.

And why don't you start by telling me your real name?"

"I would...if I could." She pivoted and grabbed his arm. "Rob, I am connected somehow to El Gringo Viejo, but I don't know how. I—I think he's trying to kill me, but I don't know why. And my name? I don't have a clue."

His gaze dropped to her hand on his arm just to make sure she didn't have the knife. She wasn't right in the head...or maybe he wasn't. Either way, he couldn't make sense of her words.

"Wait." He held up a hand as much to stop her words as to stop the thoughts swirling in his clouded mind. "I don't understand what you're telling me. If it's more lies, I don't want to hear them."

"I wish I were lying, Rob. I wish I knew enough to lie." She rubbed the side of her scalp, digging her fingers into her hair. "It must've been the head injury. I don't remember anything before waking up in that wreck. I don't know my name. I don't know who I am, and worst of all, I don't know who's trying to kill me and why."

The words tumbled from her lips in a rush, too fast for his brain to sort and comprehend. "We need to sit down."

He collapsed on a cushion of his couch, and Jane sat beside him, folding one leg beneath her—almost too close to him for rational thought.

Now that the dam had broken, she couldn't stop talking.

"I heard those men talking about killing me, and that's when I first heard of El Gringo Viejo. I had the knife in my pocket, so when you came along, I thought you might be one of them."

Placing his hands on her shoulders, he pinched his fingers into her flesh beneath the light T-shirt. "Stop. Tell me everything from the beginning…and I'll decide if I believe you or not."

She took a deep, shuddering breath and folded her hands in her lap. "The first thing I remember is coming to in the car. It was upside down. I was disoriented right from the beginning."

He barely breathed as she told him about releasing herself from the car and then hearing another vehicle arrive and voices.

"Something made me hide from those men. Alarm bells were sounding in my head." She looked up, studying his ceiling as if searching for her memories there. "I saw their shoes but not their faces. They couldn't see me at all. That's when I first heard of El Gringo Viejo."

He took his thumb out of his mouth, where he'd been gnawing on the cuticle, on the edge of his seat as she spun her story. "In what context?"

"Something about how El Gringo Viejo would be angry if they had to tell him they weren't sure whether or not I was dead."

"To be sure, they torched the car."

She nodded and drew her knees to her chest, wrapping her arms around her legs. "They thought I was still inside. Then they took off."

"Why did you hide in the desert? Why didn't you go up to the highway and wave down a car?"

"Why would I do that?" Her eyes widened. "All I knew was that someone was out to kill me, had probably forced me off the road. I didn't know who. I didn't know why. Those two men could've swung back around, and I wouldn't have even recognized them as my attackers."

"Okay, I get that you'd think that at the beginning of your…ordeal, but what about later? You had to figure they'd be long gone." He drilled his forefinger into his thigh. "And why not involve the police? Why didn't you want to go to a hospital? Get treatment? Report the accident? Tell the police about these two men?"

She hunched her shoulders. "I was afraid."

"Afraid of the police?"

"Afraid of not knowing." She tapped her head. "Do you know how it feels to have nothing up here? Of course you don't. The thought of people, strangers, coming at me and telling me who I am and where I should be…fills me with terror."

"You think your assailants would hear about the accident and the woman with amnesia and make a move?" He scratched his chin. He could understand that, but it sounded more like a movie plot.

"Can you picture it? One of them could come to the police or the hospital and tell the authorities I was his wife. That we had an argument. That he didn't know where I'd gone." She splayed her arms to her sides. "What could I say?"

She made more sense than he'd expected—not that he would've handled the situation in the same way. He tugged on his earlobe. "What about your memory loss? Where'd you get the name *Jane*?"

"Where do you think?" She stretched out her legs and kicked them up on top of the coffee table. "All I could think of while I waited in the desert was that I was a Jane Doe—no identity, no possessions, no memories. So, when you asked me for a name, that's the first one that came to mind."

"Don't you want to discover who you are? Isn't it more dangerous not knowing?"

"I didn't think so at first, but I realize it now."

He jerked his thumb toward the window.

"You're not going to find out working at Rosita's Café in a town where nobody knows you."

Her gaze dropped to her wiggling toes, and she glanced up at him through her lashes. "You know me. You're the only one who does."

"Jane, or whatever—" he clasped his hand on the back of his too-tense neck "—I don't know you. You must have family somewhere, a mother, a father, a husband…people who are worried about you."

"You think so?" She chewed on her bottom lip and examined the ring finger of her left hand, devoid of a ring or a tan line. "I don't feel married."

Rob snapped his fingers. "What about the tattoo on your back? Rosalinda? You didn't know it was there, did you?"

"Of course not."

"Where did you come up with that story about the dead girlfriend?"

"My imagination." She scooped her tawny hair back from her face. "Where else?"

"I'm just wondering if any of those names and stories you came up with have some kernel of truth to them—something coming up from your subconscious."

"I can't tell you. The only thing that resonated with me was when I told you I was an art teacher, but you already blew that theory out of the water when you told me my fingerprints aren't on file. Teachers are printed, right?"

"What about the fluent Spanish?" He shook his head. "My mother would be mortified that some gringa speaks Spanish better than I do."

"Gringa." She pulled her knees to her chest again. "Why does that man, that drug dealer, want me dead? Maybe I'm a mule, a courier, a drug dealer myself."

Rob staggered up from the couch, not wanting to think about that possibility, even though it had been at the edges of his mind ever since he saw her search history at the library. "We need a pen and paper to start writing all this down—the car, the men, the knife, the tattoo, the name. All of it."

"Does that mean you believe me?" She twisted her hair into a ponytail with one hand. "I need you to believe me, Rob. I need help."

He ducked into the office and grabbed a legal pad from a desk drawer and a pen from the holder. Returning to the living room, he drummed the pen against the pad. "I suppose someone could make up a story this crazy to infiltrate the Border Patrol or to kill me, but there would be easier ways to do that—and I've seen that gash on your head. That head injury must've stolen your memories."

Rob perched on the arm of the couch, ankle

crossed at his knee, pad of paper on his thigh. He wrote *Jane?* at the top of the page and started a bulleted list of everything she could remember.

He enlarged the dark circle next to the Rosalinda tattoo on the list. "This is the most distinct thing about you. We should take a stab at it."

"Not literally." Jane reached behind her and rubbed her lower back. "But that's what I thought when I looked in the mirror and saw myself for the first time—nondistinct. At the time, it pleased me, as I figured I could blend in, but a less bland appearance might help me figure out my identity faster."

Rob's mouth hung open. She couldn't possibly think she had a bland appearance. The color of her eyes, hair that couldn't decide between blond and brown and lush lips that turned up at the corners didn't equal mundane to him.

He muttered, "I think you lost your judgment along with your memory."

"What?" She prodded his leg.

"Never mind." He dropped the notepad on her lap and pushed up from the arm of the couch. "Now that we know Rosalinda is not the name of some murdered schoolmate, let's do another search."

He swept his laptop from the counter where it was charging and squeezed next to Jane on the couch. He launched a search engine and entered *Rosalinda* once more.

Jane ran her finger down the display. “A TV show, restaurants, people, a brand of tortillas. Do you think one of those Rosalindas could be me?”

“Only one way to find out.” Rob clicked on the first Rosalinda, which turned out to be a politician in Texas, the smile on the middle-aged blonde’s face promising more school funding and better infrastructure.

He went through all of the names, but not one of the Rosalindas matched Jane.

He slumped, tipping his head back and staring at the ceiling. “What else do people tattoo on their bodies?”

He could feel her gaze on him, assessing him in a way that heated his blood.

He rolled his head to the side. “What?”

“Do you have any tattoos, Rob?”

“No.” The word came out in a burst and Jane reeled back.

“Not a fan of inking your body, I guess.”

“Sorry, didn’t mean to snap at you.” Rob shoved a hand through his hair. “I was constantly pressured as a kid into getting the gang symbol tattooed on my arm. Both of my brothers had them. My refusal was kind of like a magical talisman in my head that assured me if I didn't get the tattoo, I'd never join the gang."

Jane squeezed his thigh. "And it worked."

"I've been tattoo-free ever since and probably always will be."

"But if you were a tattoo kinda guy, what would you get? What do your friends have? Your girlfriends?" She removed her hand from his leg and tapped her fingers on her knee.

"I don't have any girlfriends. Do you think I'd be running around with you, having you spend the night here, if I had a girlfriend?"

"You wouldn't be if *I* were your girlfriend." She brushed her hands together as if resolving that issue. "Tattoos."

If she were his girlfriend? He liked the sound of that and he didn't even know who she was.

"My buddies who were in the military have military tattoos, insignia, animals, stuff like that. The women, *not* my girlfriends, tend to have flowers, maybe little sayings, hearts." He shrugged. "Places?"

"Are there any towns called Rosalinda?" She flicked a hand at the keyboard. "We could go through each state. Rosalinda, Alabama. Rosalinda, Arkansas. Rosalinda, Arizona, of course."

"Rosalinda, Mexico." Rob clutched the sides of the laptop.

"Why Mexico?" She licked her lips and clasped her hands between her knees.

She knew.

He coughed. "Well, you speak Spanish fluently. Rosalinda is a Spanish-sounding name. We're close to the Mexican border."

"And I know El Gringo Viejo." She pressed her lips together in a straight line. "I'm not sure I want to know how well we're acquainted. Could he be my…husband? There weren't any pictures of him online."

Rob swallowed a lump in his throat. "There are no pictures of him. Nobody knows what he looks like."

"But with a name like that, *Viejo*, he has to be old…older." She interlaced her fidgety fingers. "People do have May-December relationships, though, don't they?"

He placed his hand over both of hers. He couldn't help it. "What made you think he might be your husband?"

"Because of the story I told you about escaping an abusive ex. Remember, we talked about kernels of truth."

"And remember you told me the only flicker of recognition you felt was when you said you were an art teacher." He stroked his thumb across the smooth skin on the back of her hand. "In all our years tracking El Gringo Viejo, nobody ever mentioned a spouse or partner for him."

She jabbed her finger at the monitor. "Enter it."

He typed *Rosalinda, Mexico* in the search engine and hit Return.

Jane leaned into his space, the ends of her hair tickling his hands still poised over the keyboard. "There's the TV show again. Maybe I'm just a big fan of that telenovela."

Rob eked out a breath. "Doesn't look like there's a town called Rosalinda, at least not one that rates top billing on this search engine."

"Rob." She grabbed his wrist. "There's an art gallery called Rosalinda. Right there."

He followed the direction of her trembling finger and clicked on an article from an online art blog that teased the name Rosalinda in the blurb.

He read it aloud, as Jane seemed to have been struck mute. "'For funky art pieces in a variety of media, some created by the gallery's owner, visit Rosalinda in Puerto Peñasco, better known to the gringos as Rocky Point. The proprietor and artist, Libby James, is knowledgeable about the…'"

Jane dug her nails into his flesh. "That's me. That's who I am—Libby James."

Chapter Eight

"Libby James." She said the name again, feeling it on her tongue, her lips, the roof of her mouth. "I'm Libby James."

Rob's arm went around her shoulders, and she leaned into him. "That's amazing. You remember. You can go to the police now, tell them about the accident and the men threatening you."

She stiffened. "I don't remember. I just know."

"You just know?" His arm sagged halfway down her back. "What does that mean? You don't remember your life as Libby James? Your association with El Gringo Viejo?"

She hated to disappoint Rob. He'd sounded so hopeful, so relieved that he didn't have to worry about her stabbing him in the gut while he slept.

Pounding a fist above her heart, she said, "I feel it here. I had that flash of recognition, that same flash I felt when I told you I was an art teacher. Don't you see? I *am* an artist, maybe I even teach others. The tattoo on my back is the name of my gallery."

"Maybe we can find out for sure." Rob placed his hands on the laptop's keyboard and typed in *Libby James*.

If Rob expected her face to pop up next to some biographical entry on her, he was hiding his defeat well.

Rob tapped his thumbs on the edge of the keyboard after his fruitless search. "I guess Libby James keeps a low profile."

"It makes sense, doesn't it, Rob? I'm fluent in Spanish because I live in Mexico. For the same reason, you weren't able to find my prints in your fingerprint database, or whatever it is you checked. I have the name of that gallery tattooed on my back. I *feel* artistic, and somehow I've run into, run across or run afoul of El Gringo Viejo in Rocky Point, which is a big tip for you."

"A big tip for me?" She followed his gaze as it scanned the screen, searching for her face, searching for some proof beyond her feelings.

"You all." She swiped her arm through the air. "Maybe El Gringo Viejo is in Rocky Point, too. You said law enforcement doesn't know where he is or what he looks like. Now you know he's in Rocky Point."

"I don't know, Jane." Rob rubbed his eyes and

pushed the computer from his lap onto the coffee table. "We need some kind of proof."

"Libby." She pinned her shoulders against the back cushion of the couch, feeling stronger every time she said the name. "Start calling me Libby."

"You do look more like a Libby than a Jane."

"In what way?" She tilted her head, and her hair swung over her shoulder.

"Jane… I don't know. It reminds me of plain Jane and you're anything but plain."

A tingling warmth crept into her cheeks and she pressed her hand against one side as if to stop the color she was sure had accompanied the heat.

She snorted. "Yeah, plain doesn't cut it for a woman hiding out in the desert with ripped clothing and a gash on the side of her head."

Rob rolled his eyes.

Did he think she was fishing for more compliments? Was she?

"So." She laced her fingers and stretched her arms in front of her. "What's our next step? I don't think I should go running back to Rocky Point, do you?"

"Absolutely not. If you are Libby James from Rocky Point and in some kind of trouble with El Gringo Viejo, you don't want to return to the source of your misery—especially with no understanding of what that misery is."

Rob hadn't balked at her use of *our*. Whether or not he believed her about being Libby, he wasn't going to abandon her.

"You need to get your memory back. You need to find out why those men had instructions to kill you. You need to talk to someone." He held up a finger as she opened her mouth. "Not the cops."

"I know, a psychiatrist or psychologist—someone like that. I've already been thinking along those same lines. I suppose you don't have any mental health professionals here in Paradiso."

"We do. There's a therapist who works at the hospital, and I know she sees patients outside of her work there."

She raised her eyebrows at him.

He crossed one finger over the other. "Not me. I told you I had plenty of head shrinking when I was a kid in school. I don't need any more."

"Are you sure?"

"What does that mean?"

"You rescued a knife-wielding woman in the desert and took her into your home, didn't call the cops, didn't call the hospital, didn't report the accident—some people would say you're certifiable."

"Ah, don't remind me." He buried his hands in his hair. "This cannot get out to my coworkers. They have this impression that I'm impulsive and careless."

"Do you think that's a reaction to being so very careful when you were growing up?"

His dark brown eyes narrowed. "I'll say it again. I think you're a therapist, not an artist. You have this tendency to analyze me when you're the one who needs analyzing."

"Maybe I'm just practicing for what's to come." She lifted and dropped her shoulders. "I don't need analysis so much as a swift knock on the head."

"I don't think you need that at all." He stroked his fingers over the hair covering her wound, and she melted just a little.

She sure hoped there wasn't a Mr. James out there looking for his wife.

He snatched his hand back from her head as if the same thought had just occurred to him. "If the psychiatrist at the hospital can't see you, she can recommend another therapist, although you might have to go to Tucson to see someone."

"I'd be willing to go a lot farther than Tucson to get help."

"I think your brain has done enough work

for tonight. All signs point to Libby so far, but knowing your name isn't enough. You have to remember who you are to get this straightened out."

"I agree." She rose to her feet a little unsteadily, and Rob placed a hand on her hip. "Sh-should I go back to my motel tonight?"

"No, although I was ready to kick you out after confronting you about your library searches." He left his hand on her body as if she needed propping up. Maybe she did.

"After finding out, why did you bring me back here? Why did you feed me?"

"I wanted to trip you up. I wanted to discover your motive, and then I just wanted you to tell me the truth." He ran his thumb into the pocket of her pants. "Why didn't you tell me all this before?"

"I was afraid." She lodged her tongue in the corner of her mouth. "I was afraid of the unknown, of being taken to the police station and revealed as someone who had no memory, no ID, no life. You may have thought I needed to be in the hospital, but the thought terrified me. I didn't want to be captive somewhere for some stranger to come along and claim me like a stray puppy—tell me who I was and where I needed to be."

He nodded as he stood up beside her, removing his thumb from her pocket. "I get it. It must be strange not knowing who you are, like staring into an abyss."

"Take that and multiply it by a hundred, but then you came along and didn't push even though you didn't believe me." She turned from the magnetic hold his eyes exerted on her. "I appreciate that."

"My colleagues are not completely wrong about me. I can be impulsive. I can be naive about the crime committed out here in the desert, away from the big, bad city." He stepped over the coffee table to avoid squeezing past her on his way to the kitchen. "I'll even admit that some part of me did believe your story—a woman on the run from an angry ex. I've seen enough of that in my childhood. I could relate. I could sympathize."

"I had no idea I'd be pressing your buttons with that story. It just came to me as a possibility." She pointed past him. "We didn't finish cleaning up."

"That's where I was headed." He made a stop at the table to collect the rest of their dinner. "I hate leaving a mess to clean up in the morning."

"I do, too." When Rob's head swiveled around, she held up her hand and said, "I think I do."

He tossed a dish towel over his shoulder. "I'm

sorry. I'm going to make you anxious about recovering your memories if I jump every time you make a statement about yourself."

"I don't mind. Maybe it will all come back that way." She yanked the dish towel hanging down his back. "I'll dry."

He rinsed suds from a plate and handed it to her. "Memory's a weird thing, isn't it?"

"If I didn't think so before, it's taken on a whole new dimension of weirdness for me."

"I mean—" he handed her the second plate "—you don't remember your name or where you're from or who you are, but you clearly knew where Tucson was. And you remember how to speak Spanish."

She rubbed a circle on the plate until it glowed. "Maybe the psychiatrist can explain that. I imagine it has something to do with the parts of the brain injured."

"I suppose it doesn't matter, as long as someone can help you get on track. Then we can deal with those two men…and the rest of it."

She slid a glance at his profile as he worked at the sink, his jaw tight. Was he as worried as she was at what discoveries her true identity might bring?

As she dried the last of the dishes, he sprayed some green liquid on his granite countertops and ran a paper towel over the surface until it gleamed. Was he really this particular or just stalling for time?

He didn't think she'd fall into his arms or request they share a bed for the night, did he? Would she?

She said, "You can have your T-shirt back. April even threw in a couple of nightgowns with the tags still on them."

"Yeah, she really came through." He tossed the paper towel in the trash and rubbed his hands together. "I felt kind of crummy lying to her."

She touched her fingers to her lips. "I'm sorry. That's on me. She's not the cop, right? Maybe we can tell her the truth."

"April would help anyway. It doesn't matter to her. It's not like the woman hasn't told a few lies in her time—all for the greater good, of course."

"And that's what this is, Rob—the greater good. The fewer people who know my identity, or lack thereof, the better. It'll help me keep a low profile. Can you imagine the stir an amnesiac woman would cause in this town?"

"Everyone would be talking about you for sure. I agree, the greater good."

He held out his fist for a bump, and she tapped her knuckles against his awkwardly. Were they buds now?

"Tomorrow we'll visit Dr. Escalante at the hospital for some advice. Sound good?"

"Great—sounds great." She wiped her hands on the seat of her pants, even though she'd just hung up a perfectly good towel. She backed out of the kitchen and spun toward the hallway. "Same bedroom? I mean, the same bedroom I had last night?"

Rob coughed and made a job of intricately folding a dry dish towel over the handle of the oven door. "I just have the two bedrooms. The third I use as an office."

"Yeah, yeah, that's what I mean, the room I had last night." She waved like an idiot and snatched up the pad of paper from the living room. "Okay, good night. Thanks for your help, Rob."

She rounded the corner of the hallway and stubbed her toe on the edge. She bit her lip to suppress a cry and hopped on one foot to the bedroom.

She fell across the bed on top of April's generous donation, covering her face with one arm. She hoped Libby wasn't this lame in real life.

She pushed the pile of clothes onto the floor, knowing full well Rob would have a heart attack if he saw the tangled mess on the floor—but he wouldn't be in this room. Two rooms. He had two bedrooms and this was hers, for now.

With her ear to the door, she listened to the splashing water and electric toothbrush from the master bathroom buried deep in Rob's bedroom. In the midst of it all, she slipped into a coral-hued sheath with spaghetti straps and grabbed the little plastic bag containing the toiletries she'd purchased with her first salary.

Clutching the bag to her chest, she tiptoed into the bathroom next to her room and flossed and brushed her teeth. If Libby weren't a flosser, she'd start some new habits with her new life.

Rob's cell phone rang from his room and she heard his low voice rumble in answer. Maybe it was some woman wondering why he hadn't called her back, or maybe someone he'd met on one of those online dating apps setting up a first date.

She couldn't make out his words and didn't try. The man deserved some privacy in his own home.

As she spit into the sink, he rapped on the bathroom door.

"Ja… Libby?"

Frantic eyes flew to the mirror, her gaze dropping to the skimpy nightgown clinging to and outlining her braless breasts. What was April thinking?

"Yeah?"

"Can you open the door?"

He seemed to be forcing his words through clenched teeth. Obviously, an invitation to seduction didn't wait on the other side of that door.

She placed her toothbrush on the edge of the sink and contemplated the locked bathroom door between her and the tight-voiced stranger.

"Of course. It's your door." She took a few steps on the cold tile floor and threw open the door, the smile on her lips drooping. "Wh-what's wrong?"

"The Arizona Highway Patrol found your wreck."

She placed a hand on her stomach, against the slick material of the nightgown, all thoughts of covering her jiggling breasts lost in a flood of fear. "Why'd they call you?"

"They found something in the car."

Her heart pounded, causing the silky material covering her chest to quiver. "My ID? My purse? Why would they call you?"

"They didn't find that stuff." A muscle ticked in his jaw. "They found drugs. You were hauling drugs across the border… Libby."

Chapter Nine

Her fingers curled into the nightgown at her waist, bunching and twisting it.

Did she think that evidence would be burned beyond recognition, or did she really not remember? Either way, she had drugs in the car, whether or not she remembered.

She swayed on her feet and he had an urge to catch her, pull her into his arms, but he needed to stay objective—something he'd been failing at in a big way.

She shook her head slowly at first and then so vigorously, her hair whipped back and forth like a swirl of caramel. "Nothing survived that inferno. You don't think I checked it out when the fire burned down?"

"It would've still been too hot for you to do anything more than give it a cursory look." He set his jaw, but she'd planted a seed of doubt in his mind.

She must've seen the flicker and pounced.

"You looked, too. Did you see any drugs or any packages that looked like drugs or were even intact? Pretty much everything was incinerated." She thrust out her chest and one strap of the flimsy nightgown slipped from her shoulder. "Where were they? What were they? Who found them?"

His gaze bounced from her bare shoulder to her scowling face. "Packages of meth, thrown from the vehicle. They escaped the fire. The highway patrol spotted the burned-out vehicle and went down to inspect it."

"Meth? You mean like powder?"

"Crystals. Crystal meth in plastic bags, stuffed inside a paper bag." He scratched the stubble on his chin. "About ten feet from the crash site."

"How convenient. And you believe that?" Her nostrils quivered, and a red flush stained her cheeks. "You saw that area, and believe me, so did I. I searched around the car for anything that would tell me who I was and what I was doing there, and then I searched again for water, food, crumbs. There was nothing there but trash, debris from the highway."

Rob pinched the bridge of his nose. The scene of the crash swam before his eyes—desert, sand, dirt, cactus, a few bits of highway trash, a few trees. Had he done a thorough search of the area? It had been dark, and there was no blackness like nighttime in the desert without a full moon.

He huffed out a breath. “It was dark out there.”

“I’m telling you there were no drugs.” She slammed her hand against the porcelain of the sink, and her toothbrush bounced and fell to the floor.

“What are you saying… Libby?” He dug two fingers into his temple and massaged, as if that could get rid of the pounding in his head.

“Someone planted those drugs there, Rob.” She wedged a fist against her hip, the curve of it just visible in the loose-fitting nightgown. “How did the highway patrol know about the accident? You said yourself you couldn’t see it from the highway, but you smelled it and saw the smoke. That would’ve been long gone the next morning and certainly by today. So, how’d they know it was there? Helicopter? Drone?”

He still held the phone that had brought him the bad news in his hand and he tapped the edge against his chin. “Someone reported it.”

“Aha!” She tossed her hair over her shoulder. “Don’t you see? Somebody threw the drugs out there and then called the highway patrol about the accident so they’d see the drugs.”

Libby would want to explain away the drugs so that he wouldn’t connect them to her, but her claims held more logic than desperation. He hadn't seen anything out there on the desert floor. If the drugs had been secured in the car or hidden in the trunk, how'd they get thrown in the accident?

Her version might make more sense and clear her, but the implication didn't bode well for her safety and well-being.

"You know what you're suggesting?"

Her eye twitched. "I do. The men who caused my accident came back to check their handiwork. Maybe they wondered why there was no report of a dead body found with a crash and discovered it was because there *was* no body there."

"And that means not only do they know you survived the crash, they left those drugs there as insurance to implicate you if you went to the authorities."

"It almost worked, didn't it?" She stooped to pick up the toothbrush and ran it beneath the faucet. "You charged in here to accuse me of being a drug runner, or whatever."

"Do you blame me?" He reached back to shove the phone in his pocket and realized he'd rushed in here with just his boxers on. "We still don't know anything about you."

She placed her hands on either side of the sink and leaned in to peer at herself in the mirror. "We know my name is Libby, I'm an artist and I own an art gallery in Mexico…and I'm in some kind of trouble with a drug dealer."

Feeling a sudden chill, Rob rubbed his arms. "I hope those two guys moved on after dropping those drugs…if that's what happened."

"Still doubting me? Why'd the highway patrol call you, anyway?"

"They didn't call me personally. They called the Border Patrol because of the drugs, and my supervisor called me to let me know. We have the drugs in our possession now, and you can bet I'm going to examine them for any identifying features."

"Drugs have identifying features?"

"Sure they do—consistency of product, purity of product, even packaging. That's why the highway patrol calls us." He took a step back. "I'm sorry I barged in here."

"I'm not."

He raised his eyebrows.

"I mean, I'm glad you came right to me and told me. I wish you'd done that when you discovered my search history at the library."

"You're one to talk about honesty and transparency. You didn't trust me enough to tell me you had amnesia."

"I didn't know you."

"My point, exactly." He wedged a shoulder

against the doorjamb. "Libby, what are you going to do if you find out you are involved in the drug trade somehow?"

She lifted a shoulder. "Turn over a new leaf."

He retreated to let her finish getting ready for bed. He left his door ajar and stashed his gun in the drawer of his nightstand. He was no longer worried about the strange woman with the strange story he'd picked up in the desert… He was worried *for* her.

SHE SHOT UP in the bed, panic engulfing her, her heart rattling in her chest, her dreams breaking apart and skittering in all different directions.

She placed a hand to her heart, counting the beats, breathing deeply. She still didn't know who she was beyond a name and occupation, but she felt safe for the first time since coming to in that car crash.

She had someone in the other room who believed her. Maybe Rob believed her against all his instincts and better judgment, but she'd take it.

She'd come to the conclusion that Rob could afford to be trusting and a bit impulsive because he'd honed his instincts over the years. A person didn't grow up in the conditions Rob had faced as a boy without being able to tell good from evil, without sensing danger whether it stared you in the face or crept up on you around a dark street corner.

Most people didn't have that ability, so they approached every stranger, every situation with caution and fear. Rolling to her side, she pulled the pillow against her chest. Why did she understand Rob so much better than she knew herself?

She didn't even know what kind of person she was. Was she the kind of person who could smuggle drugs across the border? Drugs that hurt kids, ruined families and destroyed lives?

No. That wasn't her. Black boots and his cohort planted those drugs to get her in trouble. To keep her from reporting the accident. And that meant they knew she was still alive.

She pulled the covers to her chin. Had they seen her in Paradiso? Had that voice she'd heard at Rosita's really been one of them?

Rob was right. She had to learn her identity sooner rather than later. And if she found out she had a husband and two children?

Her insane attraction to Rob could be based on the fact that he was the only man of her acquaintance and he'd rescued her from the desert, had even agreed not to call the cops even though he was one.

In fact, Rob Valdez was just about perfect without even taking into account his dreamy dark eyes, killer smile, hot bod and mocha skin… And he'd been beside her all night.

She hung over the side of the bed and picked up the notepad and pen she'd squirreled in her room. She couldn't sleep, so she'd stayed up sketching.

Rob's handsome face stared at her with a touch of sadness, or maybe distrust, from the top page. She flipped through the others to study the characters she'd drawn—a faceless, evil visage with silver-tipped black boots, Rosie's creased face wreathed in smiles and a fairy with curly hair and big eyes.

The knock on the door had her dropping the notepad and clutching the sheet to her chest like a virgin. For all she knew, she could be.

Rob called out in a singsong voice, "I made coffee."

"I'm awake." She kicked off the covers and dug through the clothes on the floor for a pair of sweats and a T-shirt. She didn't need to be shimmying around Rob's kitchen in the slinky nightie.

As she pulled on a pair of gray sweat shorts and a red U of A Wildcats T-shirt, she thanked the resourceful April. She'd pretty much thought of everything.

Her bare feet slapped the tile floor on her way

to the kitchen, the smell of bacon luring her in like a fish on a reel.

"I should be doing the cooking."

Rob looked up, a piece of bacon hanging from a pair of tongs over a sizzling frying pan. "You're still on the injured list."

She touched her bed-head hair. "This cut is nothing compared to the damage it did to my brain."

"While you were sleeping, I called Dr. Escalante at the hospital." He laid out the strip of bacon on a paper-towel-covered plate next to three other pieces, all running the same way, probably all equidistant, all done to the same level of crispness. He held up an egg. "Sunny-side up, over easy?"

She said without any hesitation, "Over hard with no runny yolk."

"I can do that." He cracked the egg on the edge of the skillet.

"I hope Dr. Escalante can see me and figure out why I can remember how I like my eggs but not my name or home." She grabbed the coffeepot and swirled the brown liquid in the pot. "You need a top-off?"

"I'm good." He carefully slid the crackling egg onto its other side. "Dr. Escalante referred me…you to a therapist up in Tucson. You up for a drive this afternoon after your shift at Rosita's?"

"Rosita's." She drove her heel against her forehead. "That just shows you how bad my memory is. I completely forgot about working today."

"I'm going in early to have a look at that packet of meth found near your wreck. I'll drop you off, and when you're done, we can take that ride up to Tucson. Dr. Escalante already called in your referral."

"Who's the doc?" She slurped at the black coffee, convinced she'd never taken her coffee black before in her life.

"She's not a doctor. She's a licensed therapist and hypnotist."

Libby dropped the spoon she'd just grabbed from the drawer. "A hypnotist? She's going to hypnotize me?"

"Why not?" Rob crouched down to pick up the spoon and tossed it into the sink. "What do you have to lose?"

"Not more of my memory. That's not possible." She scooped another spoon from the utensil tray and poured some milk into her coffee. "Do you think you can find out who phoned in that tip about the accident?"

"Probably not if it was anonymous, and I gather it was, but I can do some digging." He slid a couple of eggs onto a plate, alongside two perfectly placed pieces of bacon. "I'm going to do some other digging, too. I want you to know that up front. I don't want to hide anything from you, Libby."

"You're going to dig around in Libby James's background, aren't you?" She watched the swirl of milk invade coffee. "Her—my criminal background."

"If there is one, but like I told you before, your prints didn't match any we had in the database. I'm also going to make sure nobody has reported you missing."

"Is there a database that you can check in Mexico?"

"Not that we can access." He carried the plates to the table and set them down on the woven place mats. "But there are a few other places I can look. Maybe I can arm you with a little more info before your appointment this afternoon."

"Or you can arrest me."

"I don't think that's gonna happen." He pulled out a chair at the table for her and sank into the other one. He snapped a piece of bacon in two with one hand and watched it fall to his plate.

Her fork hovered over her eggs. "You're not so sure, are you?"

"It's not that, Libby." He popped one half of the bacon into his mouth. "I'm just wondering why someone felt it necessary to plant drugs at the scene of the crash."

"To shut me up."

"Then they know you're alive. How?"

"Maybe El Gringo sent them back to double-check. Maybe he sent them back to show proof of death—a picture of my charred body." She stuffed some food in her mouth so she wouldn't scream. After she swallowed and took a sip of coffee, she said, "They didn't find that proof, figured I walked away and left those drugs in case I got any ideas about ratting on them."

"Or maybe they're hanging around Paradiso and spotted you."

She leaned her fork against her plate, tines down, and folded her hands in her lap. "Thanks. You just ruined my appetite."

"I'm trying to look at all angles—no matter how ugly."

"Wouldn't you recognize a couple of strangers, thug types, wandering around Paradiso?"

Rob choked on his coffee and spit it into his napkin. "Thug types? How do you know they look like thugs? You didn't even see them."

"I thought you had superkeen instincts about these things."

"Did I say that?" He dabbed at the droplets of coffee he'd sputtered onto the table. "Sometimes thugs don't look like thugs, and sometimes people who look like thugs aren't thugs. There was a time in Paradiso, before my time, when strangers would stand out, but no longer. Not since the pecan processing plant fired up, thanks to my coworker's family. The population boomed. We have more tourism. We have more tourists coming over from Tombstone and Bisbee. Now strangers aren't uncommon. Two guys, Latinos, are not going to make waves in Paradiso."

"They could be anywhere, watching me, and I wouldn't even know it." She stared at a picture of a café on a Mexican street, a green-and-red umbrella shading a couple hunched over a small table.

"What is it? Do you remember something?"

"Just a voice at Rosita's yesterday, someone in the to-go line. It struck a chord inside, and I panicked for a minute. And then there was a guy on the street in a baseball cap." She shrugged and picked up her fork. "I suppose those events jarred me because I already realized those men could be on the loose in Paradiso."

"If they are, they must know something's going on with you. Why else wouldn't you have reported the accident, reported them? They wouldn't be sticking around to drop off a stash of meth if they were worried about that."

"They must know there's some reason why I

didn't call the cops after surviving that crash." She swallowed hard, all out of proportion to the soft eggs sliding down her throat. She didn't want to think she was involved in dealing drugs. She was sure she wasn't. Just as she knew she couldn't be so attracted to the man across from her if she were married, she knew her morals wouldn't allow her to engage in drug activity.

"The sooner you get through this morning and to that therapist appointment, the sooner we're going to figure out exactly what's going on. Once we do, I'll know how to keep you safe."

"That's important to you? Keeping me safe?" She couldn't meet his eyes, so she drew crisscross patterns on her plate with the fork.

"It's become my top priority." Rob pushed back from the table so fast, his foot caught on the leg of his chair and he stumbled. A grin lit up his face. "If I could keep myself safe first."

Libby showered and dressed in record time. When she joined Rob in the living room, she tugged on the hem of the short-sleeved, dark green T-shirt. "At least my clothes aren't ripped today."

"That's a plus." He hitched his bag over one shoulder. "If something or someone makes you feel uncomfortable at work, just leave. Rosie will understand."

She sucked in her bottom lip as she walked out the front door. "I'll be in a public place. They're not going to come in and snatch me… are they?"

"Just be careful." He helped her hop into the truck. "These cartels are ruthless. Just a few months ago, two mules were executed at the border, beheaded. They were women—Tandy Richards and Elena Delgado. They don't care."

Rob's jaw formed a hard line as he slammed the door of the truck.

Rob *did* care.

By the time he dropped her off at Rosita's, her mouth was as dry as the desert floor. Rob hadn't meant to scare the stuffing out of her, but now she'd be looking over her shoulder all morning. Better to be on the lookout instead of getting ambushed in a surprise attack.

She sauntered into Rosita's with a swagger that masked her fear—or so she thought.

"I'm glad you're back, *mija*." Rosie patted her cheek. "You look better. Is Rob taking good care of you?"

"He is." As soon as he'd stopped believing she was a drug courier like those poor beheaded women.

She waved to the guys in the kitchen and got to work. She scrutinized every male customer, her glance taking in every pair of shoes, looking for the black boots. Nobody sparked any recognition in her, and nobody acted as if she should know him.

She soon got into a groove, and the morning passed quickly. By the time she wiped the last table, Rob poked his head inside the café wearing civilian clothes—a pair of faded jeans and a light blue tee.

"Are you almost ready?"

"Not fair." She waved her towel at him. "You had a chance to clean up and change."

"I can take you back to my place if you want to shower."

She reached around and untied the apron. "That's okay. Hopefully this woman likes the smell of chips."

Rosie scurried in from the kitchen, rubbing her hands together. "Do you want some lunch, Rob?"

"No, thanks, Rosie. We're in a hurry."

Rosie patted Libby on the back. "Don't hurry this one."

He saluted. *"Sí, jefe."*

Rosie shook her head and pressed a plastic bag into Libby's hands. "You take this anyway."

Libby thanked her, and then she and Rob got into his own truck.

As he clutched the steering wheel, he said,

"That's another reason why I know you're a good person."

"Rosie?"

"You talk about my instincts. She can sniff out a phony like a bloodhound." He cranked on the engine. "She lost a son to drugs."

"Oh, no." Libby covered her mouth. "Overdose or some kind of drug violence?"

"OD. Happened before I moved here. Too bad." Rob's knuckles turned white as he squeezed the steering wheel. "Maybe I could've knocked some sense into him."

"You help enough people just by doing your job." She trailed her fingertips along his corded forearm. "You don't need to save the whole world."

"Maybe one person at a time." He threw the truck into Reverse and pulled out of the parking space. "Nothing unusual today?"

"No. You? Did you discover anything about Libby James?"

"Nothing criminal. That's quite a gallery she has down in Mexico, but she's camera shy. No pictures of her...you online."

"I guess that's not unusual. People want to see the art, not the artist." Libby gazed out the window. "I don't have much to offer the therapist."

"It's not your job to offer her anything. She's going to be helping you."

"Through hypnosis."

"You sound skeptical."

"Is she going to swing something in front of my face and tell me I'm getting sleepy?"

"That's what I mean." Rob slapped the dashboard. "You pulled that from your memory bank, and yet you can't access your personal memories."

"It's a weird condition to be in. It's like there's nothing personal there."

"There must be and this therapist—" he fished into the front pocket of his T-shirt and withdrew a slip of paper between his fingers "—Jennifer Montrose is going to help you bring it all to the surface."

About an hour later, they rolled into Tucson. They bypassed the downtown area and the university and aimed for the foothills.

Rob pointed out the window. "Looks like her office is in this business center."

Libby twisted her fingers in her lap. "What if I find out something I don't want to know about myself?"

"Whatever you find out is better than nothingness, isn't it?" He squeezed her knee. "What if you have a child somewhere?"

She flattened a hand against her belly, recalling the fairy she'd drawn last night who had borne a resemblance to her own face. "I can't. How could someone forget her own child?"

He parked the car and turned to face her. "You don't know what's going on in your head, what kind of injury you sustained. I don't think even an important memory has a chance to swim to the surface yet. That's why you're seeing Montrose."

"You're right." She released her seat belt and scooped in a deep breath. "I'm ready."

Rob checked his slip of paper for the therapist's suite number, and they walked up the stairs to the second level. When Rob tried the door with Jennifer Montrose's nameplate on the front, it swung open onto a small lobby with a few hanging plants and a blue love seat and matching chair facing each other.

Libby crept up to a closed door with a button like a doorbell on the side. Her forefinger hovered over it. "Should I?"

Rob checked his phone. "We're ten minutes early. Maybe wait until your appointment time in case someone's in there."

Libby meandered to the magazine rack and plucked up a celebrity magazine, scanning the photos on the front. Why did she recognize these people but not her own face in the mirror?

The door behind her opened, and she jumped, dropping the magazine on the floor.

"I'm sorry I startled you." The smooth, low voice alone was enough to calm her down and put her under.

Libby turned and held out her hand to the petite, dark-haired woman in the patterned palazzo pants and long blouse. "I'm Libby."

The therapist's dark eyes didn't assess her or judge. She clasped Libby's hand in a firm grip that belied her size.

"Nice to meet you, Libby. I'm Jennifer Montrose. You can call me Jennifer."

Rob introduced himself, and Libby's heart stuttered when he sank into the lone chair in the room. He wasn't going in with her to hold her hand?

Libby's eyes flew to his face and back to Jennifer's. "C-can he come in with me?"

Jennifer said, "I don't think it's a good idea, but we can do this however you want."

What if she did remember being married to El Gringo Viejo or being a drug dealer or something even worse? Did she really want Rob there to hear it all?

"No, no. Of course not. I just had a minute of panic." She wiggled her fingers at Rob, who was half out of his seat. "I'm good. I'll be fine."

"I'll be right here waiting for you." Rob winked at her.

Swallowing, she followed Jennifer into the next room, the low lights already soothing.

Jennifer took a seat in a comfortable chair. "If you want to get right to the hypnosis today, you can take the seat across from me."

"I do. That's why I'm here. I lost my memory in a car accident, and what I heard from two men after that accident has led me to believe my life is in danger. I have to find out who I am."

"I got the summary from Dr. Escalante." Jennifer tilted her head to the side, the gentle smile never leaving her lips. "You told me your name is Libby."

"Rob and I discovered a few things. I—I have a tattoo on my back, and we think it might be the name of an art gallery in Mexico owned by a woman named Libby James. No pictures, but I have a feeling about it. I also speak fluent Spanish."

Jennifer nodded. "Thank you for the information. Hypnosis is a deep state of relaxation and has been useful in the past to help people access memories. I'm going to hold up this pen and I'd like you to follow it with your eyes and listen to my voice."

After several minutes of watching the pen and listening to Jennifer's soothing voice, Jennifer's words and the feelings they evoked washed over her. Images floated across her brain—pleasant scenes of the beach and the ocean and a small gallery tucked along a cobbled street, but Jennifer pushed her away from the serenity.

What had she forgotten? What did she want to forget? What made her fearful? Who made her fearful?

The rambling villa on the coast with views forever made her stomach twist. Her feet dragged over the rolling grass. “No!”

She wanted to stop, but Jennifer’s voice prodded her onward.

She drew closer and closer to the object on the grass. Then she gripped the arms of the chair and struggled to resurface.

Jennifer led her back to awareness gently, but Libby’s heart hammered in her chest as her eyes flew open.

“He’s dead. I witnessed a murder.”

Chapter Ten

Rob sat up straight in his chair, his nails digging into the fabric on the arms as he heard a cry—Libby's cry—from the other room.

She had to go through this alone. There had to be some trauma other than the car crash that had caused her to lose her memory. Was she reliving that trauma now?

Folding his arms, he jammed his fists against his sides. He couldn't do anything for her. Could he do anything for her if it turned out she was involved with the cartels or El Gringo Viejo?

People could reform. He'd seen it before. Even his brother in prison had repented and was trying to make amends.

The door eased open, and he jumped to his feet. The doorjamb framed Libby, a tissue clutched in her hand, her eyes wide and glassy.

Jennifer hugged her. "I'll see you next week. If you need to come in before that or give me a call, please do it."

Libby shuffled toward him and plowed straight into his chest.

He wrapped an arm around her, his mouth so dry he couldn't form any words.

She mumbled against his T-shirt. "I'll tell you outside."

When they walked out of Jennifer's office, Rob squinted in the sunlight and dropped his sunglasses over his eyes.

Libby blinked, her eyes watering, until he grabbed her cheap sunglasses from the side of her purse and handed them to her. "Put these on."

She obeyed but seemed out of it. He kept a hand on her arm, not trusting her to make it through the parking lot without getting hit by a car. When they got to his truck, he nudged her inside and she plopped on the seat.

He slid behind the wheel and started the engine to get the AC running. A crease had formed between her eyebrows and she seemed to be staring at something in the distance.

Rob cleared his throat. "Do you want to tell me what happened?"

She cranked her head toward him. "I witnessed a murder."

He caught his breath. "Do you know who it was? Do you know who killed him or her?"

As horrible as the memory was for Libby, a

few knots unraveled in Rob's gut. For a minute he thought she was going to reveal that El Gringo Viejo was her vindictive spouse.

"I saw a man lying dead on the lawn. There was so much blood and I felt so much terror." She grabbed his arm, her nails digging into his flesh. "You don't think I did it, do you? Did I kill that man?"

Rob ran his hands along the steering wheel. "Was that your first feeling when you saw the body under hypnosis?"

She shook her head. "I knew he was dead, and I was afraid. Would I be so scared if I were the one who killed him? I felt a dark presence hanging over me, coming for me."

"Witnessing a murder would be enough to traumatize anyone." Rob rubbed his chin. "D-did you remember anything else? Do you know who you are?"

"I'm Libby." Her eyes widened for a second and she flipped down the visor. Scooting forward in her seat, she stared into the mirror. "I know I'm Libby James, Rob. I saw the gallery on a street in Mexico. That part was fine. It felt good…right."

"Did you remember anything else? The dead guy? His killer? Your…family?" He reached for the bottle of water in his cup holder and chugged it down so fast he coughed.

"Nothing like that." She traced a finger along her jawline as if drawing her face. "Just feelings, images, flashes of memory. Jennifer said that's completely normal and that it's a good sign I'll recover everything, eventually."

"Nothing about the car crash or the two men?" His staccato pulse returned to normal. She could handle witnessing a murder, and the fact that it shocked her was a good sign that she wasn't accustomed to the violence.

"We didn't go there. Jennifer wanted to lead me back to the events before the crash." Still watching her face in the mirror, she said, "Do you think that's why those two men were after me? Because I witnessed a murder?"

"Could be, or..." He pressed his lips together and shifted into Drive.

She jerked away from studying her reflection. "What?"

"We really don't know, do we? It's all guessing at this point. Let's wait for Jennifer." He pulled forward out of the parking space a little too fast and a car honked at him.

"You can't do that, Rob. I want all ideas on the table. Jennifer doesn't want me to wait for her. She wants me to dig whenever I can." She ran both of her hands across her face. "I'm okay. The whole hypnosis experience was strange. It rattled me, especially when I remembered that dead body on the lawn. But I'm okay."

"I'm just wondering what you were doing there with a murder victim. Were you also an intended victim? Did the killer hope to get both of you, and you escaped?" He held his breath. If she broke down, he'd have to pull over. If she returned to her semicatatonic state, he'd have to pull over. Hell, he shouldn't even be driving.

She grabbed her water bottle and shook what had to be lukewarm liquid inside. Then she screwed off the lid and took a sip. "Maybe."

His gaze slid from the road to her profile, which didn't look ready to crumble at all. "You keep talking about this lawn. Where was the man's body?"

She rubbed her bare arms. "It was on some beautiful, beachside estate—one of those lawns that runs down to the cliffs that drop off to the ocean."

"Yours?" Uneasiness stirred his belly again. Didn't much sound like the home of an artist.

"I hope not." She slammed the bottle back into the cup holder. "I don't know where it was or who owned it, but that place was pure evil. I felt that as if I were standing on the cliff's edge instead of sitting on a chair inside a therapist's office in Tucson."

"I wish this hadn't all taken place south of the

border. It would be a lot easier to track Libby James if she lived in the US. There's only so much I can do to research you if you don't have many records here."

She clapped her hands together and rested her chin on the steeple of her fingers. "But I am Libby James. I'm sure of that now, and that feels good. Thank you."

"Me?" He drove a thumb into his chest. "You were more convinced of that than I was. It's a good thing you got that tattoo. That's what led us to Libby. We would've been lost without Rosalinda."

She closed her eyes and slumped in her seat. "I feel much better now. I really do. I have a name, a place and a reason why I was on the run."

"Maybe it's time to turn this over to the authorities."

"I don't have much to give them, Rob, and there are those drugs at the accident scene." She clasped her hands between her knees. "I don't want anyone else providing the narrative of my life before I have a chance to remember it."

With what she could give them now, the cops most likely wouldn't believe she had anything to do with the drugs in her car. He clenched his teeth. Yeah, they might. When he questioned a suspect, he came in with a healthy dose of skepticism, and Libby's story sounded outlandish on the surface.

He didn't know what had happened to that skepticism when he first came across Libby. Maybe it was the fear in her eyes. The story of abuse. Maybe it was the knife she was wielding.

She poked him in the ribs. "Why are you grinning? Are you thinking about my explanation to the cops about what happened?"

"Sort of."

"I hope you agree it's too early."

"I'm not going to force you to do anything you're not ready to do…except eat dinner." He patted his stomach. "I'm starving, but I can wait until we reach Paradiso."

"Maybe by then I'll have an appetite. Seeing that dead man—" she hunched her shoulders and a tremor shook her frame "—was almost like seeing him in person. In fact, it was all so real."

He stroked her arm with one knuckle. "I'm glad Jennifer helped you. Maybe that session unlocked the door, and the memories will keep flowing."

"I hope so." Closing her eyes, she scrunched down in the seat and leaned her head against the window.

Maybe she was trying to access more memories or maybe she was just sleeping. Either way, he left her alone for the rest of the drive back to Paradiso.

She didn't stir until he signaled to take the exit into town. She dragged her hand across her mouth and blinked. "Are we back yet?"

"Pretty much. Do you want to stop off and change?"

She yawned. "Are you still starving?"

"Ravenous." His eyes flicked over her body as she uncurled and stretched out.

"Then let's eat." She rubbed her chin. "Any drool?"

Just his own.

"No drool. You look refreshed." He reached over and tucked a strand of hair behind her ear. "Do you feel better about what you learned under hypnosis?"

"Anything, especially something that doesn't point to my involvement in the drug trade, is going to make me feel better at this point." She powered down her window a crack. "Of course, I don't know who that poor murdered man was."

"Do you remember what he looked like?" He hadn't wanted to upset her before by asking any details, but she'd calmed down and those details were important.

She screwed up one side of her face. "He was old. He had gray hair…matted with blood. I couldn't tell you his height because he was lying on the ground."

"Latino? White guy?"

"White—gringo." She clapped a hand over her mouth. "You don't think that was him, do you? El Gringo Viejo?"

"That wouldn't make sense if the two guys were afraid to tell him they hadn't confirmed your death. If he were dead himself, he wouldn't care." He pulled onto Paradiso's main drag. "Burgers and fries or something more elegant?"

She pinched the material of her khaki-colored capris between her fingers. "Do I look elegant?"

"You look…fine."

"What if the man in my memory wasn't dead? What if he were just injured? He could still be El Gringo Viejo." Straightening in her seat, she pushed the hair from her face. "What if I injured him? That would be motive for him to come after me."

Rob rolled his eyes. "You're determined to make yourself the bad guy, aren't you? Your first impression of the man in your image was that he was dead—murdered."

"Maybe I thought I'd killed him but didn't. So, in my memory he'd be dead because I wouldn't have known any better."

He pulled the truck up to the curb of the Paradiso Café and cut the engine. "And why would the owner of an art gallery try to kill a drug supplier?"

"Argh, I don't know." She drilled her finger in the middle of her forehead. "This is what I come up with when I think about my past. You have to admit, my life has been pretty dramatic up to this point. Also, an American living in Mexico, running an art gallery with a drug dealer after her, has to be an adventurous person. Would you agree with that?"

"I would, but your association with El Gringo Viejo, if there is one, could be purely innocent, unintentional." He snatched his keys from the ignition. "Look, I know a lot of people in my old neighborhood who were not looking for trouble and got swept up in it anyway. Rocky Point may be a tourist area, but it's also on the edge of an area controlled by the Las Moscas and Sinaloa cartels. If you wander in the wrong neighborhood, you could be in a world of hurt."

She cocked her head. "I like that you're more optimistic about my background than I am. Rob Valdez, you're an optimist. Despite everything, you're still an optimist."

"I'd say I'm an optimist *because* of everything." He pushed open the door of his truck. "Let's eat."

As usual, she'd hopped out before he could get her door. He still went around to the passenger side of the truck and took her arm as they walked into the restaurant.

Being a little early for dinner, they had their choice of tables, and Rob led Libby to one by the window.

He snatched up two plastic menus from the side of the table as he sat down, sliding one over to her side. "They have more than burgers here, but the burgers are good."

She trailed her finger down the menu. "A burger sounds good."

"I'm going to have a beer, too."

"Me, too."

He raised his eyebrows at her. "Are you sure?"

"Who knows? Maybe if I get rip-roaring drunk, everything will come back to me. Jennifer explained that hypnosis puts you in a deeply relaxed state." She flicked her finger against the menu. "Maybe beer will do the same."

Sydney, the waitress, scurried over even though she had just two other tables. "You're early, Rob." Her gaze wandered to Libby, but he didn't feel the need to make introductions. Sydney could get her info like everyone else—from the town grapevine.

He pointed to Libby. "Are you going to order that beer?"

Libby picked out an IPA on draft and ordered a burger with avocado.

"Good choice." He ordered the same beer and a double-bacon burger.

Sydney returned minutes later with two frosty mugs of beer.

Libby planted her elbows on the table. "What am I keeping you from?"

He slurped his drink through the foamy head and asked, "What?"

"You've been babysitting me for two days now, got some clothes for me, took me to Tucson. What should you be doing instead and with whom?"

"I told you I didn't have a girlfriend." He licked his lips and gulped back more beer.

"You don't have any friends? Hobbies? Commitments?" She wrapped her hands around her own mug and took a delicate sip, which left foam on her upper lip.

Before he could make a fool of himself and wipe it off for her, she dabbed her mouth with a napkin.

"I've been with the Border Patrol just over a year. I just passed probation a few months ago. I didn't even live in Paradiso until a month ago. I was waiting to pass probation before making the move from Tucson."

"You commuted here all the way from Tucson?"

"Just in case I didn't make the department, I wanted to be in a place where I could look for other work."

"That's why your house is so neat. You haven't been there long."

"Yeah." He felt the warmth creep up to his hairline. He'd let her believe that instead of revealing his control-freak tendencies. Maybe that was why he'd jumped on her case. He'd wanted to control what happened to her. Better keep that to himself. The poor woman had enough problems.

"So—" she ran a fingertip along the rim of her mug "—it's not because you like to control all aspects of your life because you had so little control as a child?"

Shaking his head, he said, "I'm telling you. You should hang your shingle right next to Jennifer's."

Sydney returned to their table with two baskets containing their food.

Rob pointed a French fry at Libby, attacking her burger. "Hypnosis must've made you hungry."

She circled her finger in the air while she chewed, and then said, "Once I got past the shock of seeing that dead man, I started to feel a lot better. Just confirming that I'm Libby James did me a world of good."

Rob kept his mouth full because he didn't want to rain on her parade by reminding her that the hypnotic state hadn't confirmed her identity.

She'd made an assumption based on the art gallery and feeling at home there.

He hadn't seen her eat with such gusto since he'd picked her up in the desert, so he swallowed and stuffed another few fries in his mouth.

As they finished up their meal and Rob reached for his wallet, a dark-haired man stormed through the door of the café, his mouth agape and his eyes wide. Rob's muscles coiled, as the man made a beeline for their table.

"Mel!" The man tripped to a stop and made a grab for Libby's hand, which she jerked away from him.

"Mel, what's wrong? Thank God I found you. I've been searching the hospitals, everywhere."

Libby put her hands in her lap and hunched her shoulders. "Who are you? My name's not Mel."

The man's jaw dropped open, and his gaze flew from Libby's face to Rob's. "What do you mean, Mel? What's happened to you? Who's this man?"

Libby swept her tongue over her lips. "My name's not Mel. It's Libby, Libby James."

The man started to laugh and then choked. "What's going on here? Where have you been?"

"Hold on a minute." Rob stood up, towering over the shorter man with the ponytail. "Who are you? How do you think you know Libby?"

The man's dark eyes glittered, and a flush

spread beneath his brown skin as he squared his shoulders.

"I don't *think* I know her. She's my wife, and that's—" he jabbed his finger in the air at a petite Latina holding a gurgling baby "—our baby."

Chapter Eleven

Libby swiveled in her seat to take in a young woman with an infant clinging to her side. The room spun, and she grabbed the edge of the table. "I—I'm not…"

She lost the words in a haze of confusion and despair, slumping against the vinyl banquette.

"Are you all right?" Rob shoved a glass of water toward her. "Drink this."

The man with the ponytail braced his hands on the table, leaning toward her, invading her space. "What kind of joke is this? What's going on?"

Rob held up his hand. "Back off a minute. Let's take this conversation outside."

Her so-called husband's hand formed into a fist, and he banged on the table. "Who are you to give me orders? Why are you with my wife? Where has she been the past two days?"

"I'll explain everything once we get outside." Rob tossed some bills on the table. He reached out a hand to Libby under the glare of the man with the ponytail, and then stuffed it in his front pocket. "Are you okay, Libby? Can you get up by yourself?"

The man snorted. "She's not Libby James, and what's wrong with you, Mel? Why can't you move on your own?"

Stepping closer to the man, Rob dipped his head. "She's been in an accident. We'll talk outside. Get out of her space."

Libby grabbed her purse and hitched it over her shoulder, gripping the strap. Rob didn't believe this man, did he? Because she didn't…not for one minute.

Her gaze strayed to the sweet-faced young woman bouncing the baby. The girl gave her a shy smile and said, "*Hola*, Senora Bustamante."

Libby shook her head and covered her eyes with one hand. She wasn't married to this man. She didn't have that baby with him. He hadn't been in her recovered memories.

As she rose from the table, the stranger put his hand on her back, and she twitched.

He blinked his long lashes. *"Mi querida."*

She wasn't his dear or anyone else's. She longed to fall into Rob's arms right now, collapse against his broad chest. But she straightened her spine and walked away from both men, giving the baby a wide berth.

The eyes of the other customers tracked their

progress out of the restaurant as Sydney called after them, waving the two twenties. "Thanks, Rob."

Out on the sidewalk, Rob took charge again. "There's a park across the street. Let's get the baby some shade."

"You took control of my wife, and now you want control of my baby, too?" The fake husband puffed up his chest.

"I'm not taking control of anyone." Rob dragged his wallet from his pocket and flipped it open. "If it makes you feel any better, I'm Border Patrol."

The man's eyebrows jumped to his hairline. "Is it the drugs? They're not ours."

Libby cleared her throat and found her voice. "Stop. Talking."

"It's not about any drugs." Rob curled his fingers into his hair. "There, on the bench under the tree."

When they got across the street, Rob placed his hand on the young woman's arm. *"Como se llama?"*

"Teresa."

"*Sientate, aquí con la bebe*, Teresa." Rob patted the back of the bench, and Teresa sank down, cuddling the baby in her lap.

"Your Spanish stinks." The man's lip curled, and Rob rolled his eyes.

"Yeah, I know." He turned to Libby and asked

her if she wanted to sit down, with less solicitation in his voice than he'd had for Teresa.

Was he already starting to distance himself from a woman he thought was another man's wife? But she wasn't Senora Bustamante. He had to believe that.

She declined to sit and held on to the back of the bench for dear life instead. If Rob believed this man, she didn't want him framing her story, either. She had to grab hold of this narrative before it careened out of control.

She took a deep breath. "I was in a car accident. I had a head injury and lost my memory but I've already been under hypnosis to regain it, and I know I'm Libby James. I'm not married. I don't have any children."

"Thank you. That explains it." The man closed his eyes and placed his hands together. "I'm Pablo Bustamante, and you're my wife, Melissa Bustamante. This is our daughter, Luisa. We live in Rocky Point, as the American tourists call it, and you work at an art gallery—for Ms. Libby James."

Libby felt the world tilt again and dug her feet into the gravel beneath her. "I—I don't know you."

"Mi querida." Pablo put his hand over his heart. "That destroys me."

"Wait a minute." Rob's voice, rough around the edges, cut through Pablo's sadness...or feigned sadness. "What's your story? Why was your wife traveling in a car by herself up to the US?"

Pablo folded his arms. "We were taking a trip up north. Mel went in a different car to look at some art pieces. We were all going to meet up later in Tombstone, but Mel never showed up. Last I knew, she was heading up to the Paradiso area. When it seemed that her cell phone went dead and she wouldn't call me, of course I got worried. I came down here to look for her, checked the hospitals, called the police. I couldn't figure out what happened. Now that you tell me you lost your memory, Mel, it adds up, and I'm so relieved even if you don't remember me."

"I don't." Libby set her jaw, refusing to look at the sweet baby now tapping Teresa's face with her little fist. "Wait."

"Do you remember, *mi querida*?" Pablo stretched a hand out to her, adding a slight tremor for maximum effect.

"No, I don't remember, and neither does Luisa." She leveled her finger at the baby. "She seems much more interested in and engaged with Teresa than me. If I were truly her mother, wouldn't she be more excited to see me?"

Rob cranked his head back and forth, looking at the baby, a smile lighting up his face. "She has a point there, Pablo."

Pablo's eyes flashed for a second when he glanced at Teresa and Luisa. "Teresa is her nanny. This has been an issue between us before, Mel. Besides, this is stupid. Why would I come around and try to claim a stranger as my wife?"

"Good question." Rob's eyes narrowed.

"This is ridiculous. You're coming home with us, Mel, and we'll sort all this out when we get there. I'll introduce you to the real Libby James—your boss." He lunged forward and grabbed her arm.

Rob reacted with lightning speed, stepping between them and breaking Pablo's hold on her with a single, swift chop to the other man's arm.

Pablo gave a strangled cry and stumbled back while Teresa jumped up, clutching Luisa to her body.

As Pablo righted himself, his hands curled into fists at his sides.

"Don't try it." Rob flattened his hand across his body, revealing the outline of his weapon holstered on his hip. "I don't know what kind of game you're playing here, but if you think Libby is going to traipse off with someone she doesn't know to go God knows where, you don't know her at all and you sure as hell don't know me."

"You can't keep me from my wife." Pablo's lips curled into a snarl, the concerned husband and father disappearing.

"Even if she is your wife, which I doubt, she'll make her own choices about what she wants to do." Rob pulled out his phone. "If you want to give me your middle initial and birth date and any other identifying information, I'll run you and see if your story is true."

"Run me?" Pablo put his hand on the baby's back. "You're Border Patrol. I'm not giving you any information."

"Better yet, come down to the station with me and we'll fingerprint you. We should be able to confirm your identity, and then you and… Mel can work things out together, if she wants to. We can even call the gallery and speak to Libby James about her employee."

Rob shoved one hand in his pocket, as if his request were the most natural thing ever, and wasn't it? Wouldn't a distraught husband be anxious to prove who he was?

Pablo said in a low voice, "I'm not doing that. Won't you just hold her, Mel?"

"Sure." Libby flipped her hair over her shoulder and held out her arms to Teresa.

The young woman slid a glance to Pablo, who gave her an almost imperceptible nod. She then peeled Luisa from her body and put her in Libby's arms.

Libby tucked one arm beneath the baby's bottom and patted her back, her baby-powder smell tickling her nose. "Hi, precious. What a sweet girl you are."

Luisa's dark eyes widened and her bottom lip quivered. She placed her little hands against Libby's chest and squirmed.

"It's okay." Libby stroked the baby's soft curls. "Are you looking for Teresa?"

Teresa started forward, but Pablo grabbed her upper arm, pinching her flesh.

Libby turned around so that Luisa could see Teresa and immediately the baby started to whimper and kick her legs against Libby's belly. "I know, sweetie. You want Teresa."

She poured the baby back into Teresa's willing arms and spun around on Pablo, her eye twitching. "That's not my baby. I don't know who you are or why you want me, but I'm not going with you…or anyone else."

"Mel! This is not over. I'll prove you belong with me."

Libby strode away from the little group under the tree on shaky legs. Rob caught up with her as she crossed the street and grabbed her hand.

"Are you all right?"

"Let's just keep walking to the truck. I'm going to collapse in the middle of the street if I stop moving."

When Rob handed her into the truck, she twisted her head over her shoulder. Pablo was waving his arms around and Teresa had sat back down with the baby, who looked as if she were crying. Libby shivered.

Rob slammed the door and gripped the steering wheel. "What the hell was that all about?"

"It's what I feared from the get-go." Libby folded her hands in her lap and dropped her gaze. "Someone coming forward claiming to know me. Some stranger taking me away."

"I'm not going to allow that to happen." He wedged a finger beneath her chin, tipping up her head. "Look at me."

She slid her gaze to the left, meeting his dark eyes burning with…some emotion she couldn't name.

"You're not going anywhere with anyone, unless and until you want to. You're not going to take some dude's word for it that you're married and have a child if you don't remember that marriage or that child."

"C-couldn't you have arrested him or something?"

"Nothing he did was a crime." Rob lifted his shoulders. "And while I wanted to punch him in the face when he grabbed you, I would've been the one arrested."

"What kind of a person would use an innocent child like that?" Libby shook her head. "I could tell Teresa, or whatever her name is, was scared out of her wits. Didn't you think?"

"I think—" Rob cranked the keys in the ignition "—Teresa is that baby's mother and Pablo was using both of them to lure you into his trap."

Libby pulled her bottom lip between her teeth. "He's not one of the men at the crash site, though. I'm sure of it—different voice. That means there are more than two. Pablo must be working with the others, and they must know I have amnesia."

"He wouldn't have approached you otherwise with that story, but he didn't seem surprised when you mentioned Libby James and he knew Libby—you— Sorry, this is getting confusing. He knew you owned a gallery." Rob pulled away from the curb and headed in the opposite direction of his house.

Libby's heart skipped a beat. "We're not going back to your place?"

"I'm going to check out the Paradiso hotels first and find out where Pablo and Teresa are staying—and how they registered."

"Good idea." She twisted a lock of hair with her finger, let it go and wound it up again. "How did Pablo know I had amnesia? Only you, Jennifer and I know that. Not even Rosie knows it."

"Maybe they've been watching you. If you knew who you were and who they were, you'd report their actions or you'd continue to do what you were planning to do before they waylaid you."

"They planted those drugs at the accident scene to make sure I didn't report anything, or if I did, that I'd be arrested for those drugs."

"You drove up here to Paradiso for a reason—maybe it has to do with that dead body in your memory and maybe not. They stopped you but would've expected you to carry on with your mission…if you knew what it was." He tapped on his window as they rolled up to the Paradiso Motel. "They knew something was wrong when you stayed here and took a job at Rosita's. Now they know for sure because my guess is that you're no stranger to Pablo Bustamante."

She'd accept his explanation for now, but the notion that people who meant to do her harm were watching her in Paradiso did nothing to calm her nerves.

The clerk at the Paradiso Motel didn't have anyone matching Pablo's and Teresa's descriptions staying there, and Libby and Rob didn't have any luck at the other two hotels, either.

After the visit to the last hotel, Libby climbed into Rob's truck and snapped her seat belt with a sigh. "At least we tried. I guess we can do a search on Pablo Bustamante, just like we did on Libby James, but I don't know how much we'll find."

"Well, I did get his fingerprints."

Libby jerked her head around. "You did?"

Rob pulled a pacifier from his pocket. "Like taking candy from a baby."

"You stole little Luisa's binky?" She punched his arm.

"Not exactly. It fell out of her mouth onto the ground. Pablo picked it up, left fingerprints and handed it back to Luisa, who promptly dropped it again. Pablo didn't notice this time, so I scooped it up with a tissue and pocketed it." He held up his hands. "Don't get too excited. We could have the same issue we had with your prints. If he's a Mexican national, his prints aren't going to be in our database. I have to go through other red tape to get that information, and nothing I'm doing is official at this point."

"It's a start. I never would've thought of that." She scooted down in the seat. "I'm exhausted. Just when I thought I unwound from my session with Jennifer, I get hit with Pablo. Did he really think I'd just waltz off with him?"

"He obviously thought the baby would be the clincher." He raised an eyebrow. "She *was* cute. How'd you resist?"

"Cute? She was adorable, but I knew she wasn't mine. I had no feeling for her here." She pounded her fist against her heart. "I'd know. I'm sure I'd remember a baby…or a husband."

"You'd like to think you would, but who knows?" He slowed down to make the turn to his street. "I knew she wasn't yours by the way she clung to Teresa and barely looked at you. One of the other agents and his fiancée are adopting a baby, and that little guy is constantly zeroed in on his mama no matter who else is holding him. Luisa didn't have that for you."

"I agree." Libby shot up in her seat. "You have a visitor."

Rob rolled past the Jeep parked in front of his house and pulled into his driveway. "Friend, not foe."

Libby blew out a breath and threw open the passenger door before Rob even cut the engine. She could do with more friends and fewer foes.

A tall woman with a thick mane of blond hair and sun-kissed skin stepped out of the Jeep and waved. "Those pants actually look better on you than they ever did on me."

Libby stumbled and made a grab for the door of the truck. "I know you."

Rob came around to her side of the truck and hugged the blonde. "I should hope so. This is April Archer, your clothing fairy."

The adrenaline rushed through Libby's body, and she swayed on her feet. "No, I know this woman…from before."

Chapter Twelve

April glanced at Rob, a crease forming between her eyebrows. "Is she okay, Rob?"

Rob lunged back toward Libby, as she listed to one side. He caught her arm and steadied her. "Are you sure, Libby? This is April Archer, Border Patrol agent Clay Archer's wife. She's the one who loaned you the clothes."

April charged forward. "Rob, she needs to sit down. She needs water or a stiff drink. We can sort this out inside."

Rob knew better than to get into a struggle with April over taking care of someone. She was the pro.

Libby let April curl an arm around her shoulders and guide her to the house, so Rob sprang ahead of them to open his front door.

April walked Libby to the couch and patted a cushion. "Sit and tell me what's going on. Water? Tea? Whiskey?"

"Maybe some water." Libby rubbed the side

of her head where her external wound was healing nicely. Soon there'd be no outer sign of her memory loss—just the vast emptiness inside her head.

"Rob." April snapped her fingers. "A glass of water."

Rob rushed into the kitchen and filled a glass with filtered water from the fridge. When he returned to the living room, April was seated next to Libby, whose face had returned to its normal shade.

April asked in a soft voice, "You think you know me from somewhere? Why does that worry you? Do you think I know your ex?"

Libby dropped her head back against the couch, staring at the ceiling. "Rob told you that story?"

"Story?" April glanced at Rob. "Is it a story? Whatever your story, you can tell me. No judgment."

Libby closed her eyes, and her chest rose and fell rapidly. "I don't have an abusive ex, or at least not that I know of. I was in a car accident the other day outside Paradiso, and I lost my memory. Rob's been helping me, and we've pieced together a few things."

"A car accident?" April tucked one long leg beneath her. "That burned-out wreck off the highway?"

"That's the one." Libby opened one eye.

"The accident found with the drugs?"

"Not hers." Rob perched on the edge of the chair across from them.

"Is that why you didn't report it? Get help?"

"Not at first, but those drugs haven't made it any easier." Libby launched into an explanation of the accident and the two men who set fire to the car.

"Oh, my God. You poor thing." April grabbed Libby's hand. "You still need to get checked out by a doctor. Rob, what were you thinking?"

"Don't blame Rob." Libby's gaze shifted to him, and his heart melted around the edges. "He was trying to protect me."

April asked, "So, where do I fit in? How do you know me, or how do you think you know me because I don't know you, Libby."

Rob hunched forward, his elbows digging into his knees.

Libby massaged her left temple. "I've never met you. I've never seen you in person, but I've seen a photograph of you."

Sitting back, Rob rolled his shoulders. "You probably saw a picture of her that I had somewhere. I told you. She's married to a fellow agent—my boss."

"That's not it, Rob. I didn't see a picture of

April since I've been here in Paradiso. I saw it before...before I lost my memory."

"You saw a picture of her somewhere in Rocky Point, Mexico?"

"Rocky Point? That's where you're from?" April rubbed her chin. "That's cartel country. I wonder if my ex-fiancé..."

"Your ex-fiancé is a drug dealer?" Libby blinked her wide eyes.

"Was. He's dead." April waved her hand in the air. "Long story. Why did someone plant drugs at the scene of your accident? My husband told me those were packaged to sell."

"I hope I don't have an ex-fiancé who's a drug dealer, but I am mixed up somehow with those people." Libby pinned her hands between her knees and hunched her shoulders. "The two men who set fire to my wrecked car mentioned something about some guy called El Gringo Viejo. I've since discovered he's some sort of broker for the cartels."

April's lips formed an O, and she clutched her midsection. "El Gringo Viejo?"

Rob raised his eyebrows. Clay must share everything with his wife. He'd remember that the next time his boss got on his case. "Clay mentioned him to you before?"

"Not just Clay." April jumped up from the couch and did a circle around the room. "My brother, Adam, mentioned El Gringo Viejo to me long before I heard about him from Clay."

"Your brother." Rob cleared his throat. "He's the one who, yeah, had some problems with drugs?"

"He had a lot of problems, Rob, not just with drugs, but you know my history in this town, don't you?"

"I know your brother murdered your mother and let your father take the blame for it." Rob ignored Libby's sharp intake of breath. "I know your father disappeared after the murder and hasn't been seen since."

"Do you also know that Adam was convinced our father was El Gringo Viejo?"

"What?" Libby pushed up from the couch and grabbed April's arm. "Are you serious?"

"Wait, wait." Rob dragged a hand through his hair. "I never heard that your father, C. J. Hart, was suspected of being El Gringo Viejo. We don't know who he is. Nobody does."

"That's because I'm the only one, except Adam and he's dead, who suspects it. Clay dismissed Adam's rantings as wishful thinking, and, of course, he strongly advised me against going to Mexico to investigate the matter."

"What makes you think he's your father?" Libby dropped her hand from April's arm and stooped to grab her glass of water from the coffee table.

"Besides my brother telling me he was?" April flicked her hair over her shoulder. "The timing of my father's disappearance matches the emergence of EGV. Authorities are convinced my father slipped across the border after my mother's murder. My father had been dabbling in the drug trade before the murder, which is how my brother was able to convince him to go on the run. And, well, he's an old white guy."

"And now maybe I have further proof." Libby chugged down some water and offered the glass to April, who shook her head. "If I knew El Gringo Viejo in Rocky Point and he had your picture somewhere, it makes sense that I'd see it and recognize you from that picture."

"I'm glad you two have this all figured out." Rob rubbed his eyes. Was Libby imagining things? She still didn't remember her own name.

"I'm telling Clay about this. He's never believed this story about my father."

"Wait." Rob sliced his hand through the air. That was all he needed—his boss coming down on him because he'd gotten April involved in some wild-goose chase for El Gringo Viejo. "This is not proof. Did you miss the part where Libby told you she had amnesia? She could've seen you anywhere in town. She's working at Rosie's now."

April wedged a hand on her hip. "I haven't been to Rosie's this week, and I'm not going to drag you into it, Rob."

"I'm already dragged in. Libby's staying at my place. I rescued her from a burned-out wreck in the desert, and I didn't report that burned-out wreck to the authorities. How do you think that's gonna go over with Clay?"

"I'll handle Clay." April patted Libby's shoulder and smiled. "You guys have been speculating about EGV for years, and Libby and I may have just handed him to you."

Libby's eyes widened. "You don't mind that he's your father?"

"Might be." Rob pushed up from the chair. "Might be and probably isn't."

April gathered her hair in one hand, holding it back as she tilted her head to look him in the face. "I've lived with the idea of my father killing my mother and abandoning us for so long, this twist won't come as a shock."

"The only way we're going to know for sure is if someone goes down to Rocky Point to investigate, and that's not gonna be Libby—not for a while." He folded his arms and puffed out his chest in case there was any doubt he meant business.

April drummed her fingers on his forearm. "Ooh, I like a man who's large and in charge, especially when he's protecting his woman."

"Libby's not… I mean, of course I'm protecting her. She's vulnerable." He narrowed his eyes at April, the troublemaker. "Why exactly did you stop by, anyway?"

She winked at Libby. "Just to see how the clothes were working out and if *your friend* needed anything else. Do you, Libby?"

"You were more than generous, and I, for one, am glad you came by."

"Nobody handles Clay Archer, not even you, April."

"Don't worry about it." She floated to the front door and blew them a kiss before she left.

"That was strange." Libby dropped to the couch and covered her face with both hands. "When I saw her, it was like an immediate flash of recognition. It's happening, Rob. If I went back to Rocky Point and my gallery, I'm sure the memories would start rolling in."

He swallowed. He had no right to keep her here, but he'd do everything in his power, short of physical restraint, to persuade her not to return to Mexico. "I hope you realize going to Rocky Point would be the most dangerous move you could make right now. It's a catch-22, but regaining your memory is going to put you at risk."

"After that showdown with Pablo, they know for sure I don't have any memory of what I was doing in that car on that road. I'm safe…for now." She patted the cushion on the couch beside her. "Sit. Did I thank you for protecting me against Pablo?"

He lowered himself next to her. "I think you handled it."

"Only because you were there." She ran a hand down his thigh. "He wasn't about to try anything with you there. If you hadn't been…"

He cinched his fingers around her wrist, more to stop her hand traveling up his thigh than anything else. "I was there. I am here, and I'm going to see you through this."

Her bottom lip trembled. "I don't know how I got so lucky that you were the one who found me. If it had been anyone else, any other authority figure, my face would be plastered all over town or I'd be in jail for those drugs."

"I don't think so." He raised her hand to his lips and kissed the tips of her fingers, immediately regretting it. What kind of man took advantage of a woman with no identity? He didn't even know if she were free.

He loosened his clasp on her hand, but she curled her fingers around his thumb.

"Why stop?" Her whispered words echoed in his head, as if they'd come from his own brain.

"You know why. It's not a good idea for us to…hook up."

"It seems like a really good idea to me right now." She scooted in closer to him. "You're my anchor, Rob."

"I'm your only acquaintance. Of course you're going to feel this way about me."

She snorted lightly, her nostrils flaring with the effort. "Rosie is an acquaintance. April is an acquaintance now. I spent an intense hour with Jennifer today."

"They don't count. They're all women, and you're not living with them." He traced the curve of her neck with his fingertip. "You want comfort. I understand. It must be scary as hell to be where you are right now. I get it."

Turning her head, she pressed a kiss on his palm. "I don't think you get it at all, Rob. I'm attracted to you. I like you, and, yeah, it would feel great to be connected to someone, but not just anyone. I'm sure Pablo would've been more than willing to…connect with me. You're not just some port in a storm, my particular storm. You're Rob Valdez and I want *you*."

"Libby, what if you're married?" He clasped the back of his neck. "You saw that baby today. What if you had one of those, or two? A worried husband? A frantic boyfriend? I know I'd be in a panic if I lost you."

"You're not going to lose me." She cupped his face with her hand and toyed with his earlobe. "I'm not with anyone in my real life, Rob. I know that as much as I know I'm Libby James, as much as I know I saw a dead body, as much as I know I've seen April Archer's picture somewhere."

"Bad comparisons. As tenuous as your memories are of those things, you still have some proof or image that they're true. Just because you haven't had any flashes of memory about a husband and children, it doesn't mean they don't exist out there."

Sighing, she closed her eyes. "You don't want to make love with me because you're worried we're cheating on some nameless, faceless person who probably doesn't exist?"

Was he? He didn't like making mistakes in his life. He'd worked hard to avoid missteps. Falling for someone else's wife was not in his life plan.

But neither was picking up a strange woman and making all her problems his own.

He draped his arm around her shoulders and pulled her close. He whispered in her ear, "There's no hurry, is there? When you get your memory back and know for sure you're single, we have time to explore if that's what you still want."

She nestled her head in the crook of his neck. "You don't have to be careful with me, Rob. In fact, I'm the last person you need to be careful with. I'm nobody. I'm a woman without a past and not much future."

"You're somebody to me." He rested his cheek against the top of her soft hair. "And you're worth protecting."

She curled her legs beneath her and slanted her body across his, wrapping one arm around his waist. Her hair fanned out across his chest and he took a strand between two fingers and ran them down to the ends.

Her body felt warm against his, and her breathing deepened. The bed was still made up for her, but he didn't want to move her. Didn't want to move himself. Didn't want to breathe.

He held her and looked down at her profile, studying every curve and her delicate bone structure. In sleep, her face lost its haunted look. Even when she smiled, it didn't light up her eyes. It was as if she had to know who she was, who she'd been, before she could allow herself to just be.

He knew her desire to have sex with him came from a need to get lost in her feelings, a chance to stop thinking.

When he made love to Libby James, he wanted to be with the real Libby, someone who could give him all of herself unreservedly because she knew exactly who she was and what she wanted.

Would he ever have that chance? Was Libby James a married woman? Engaged? In love? He could wait to find out. For now, he had this. He ran his hand down her back.

She arched like a cat, and then burrowed into his chest.

He could sleep with her next to him like this all night…and probably would. Closing his eyes, he tilted back his head.

A few minutes later, or maybe it was a few hours, someone pounded on his front door and a woman's cry pierced through the haze of sleep. He jerked forward, his arms going around Libby.

Thank God she was safe. Just as his heart rate returned to normal, he heard the cry again and the glass in his front door shook.

Libby sat up, blinking. "What was that?"

"Someone's at the door." He put his finger to his lips and scooted out from beneath Libby, still halfway draped across his lap.

He reached for his weapon on the end table next to the couch and staggered to his feet, shaking off the cobwebs of sleep.

Libby grabbed the back pocket of his jeans. "Be careful."

Rob crept to his door and stood to the side. With his gun raised, he flicked aside the curtain and swore. "It's Teresa...and she has the baby."

Libby stumbled against his back, her hand to her throat. "Is Pablo with her?"

"Not that I can tell."

"It's a trick, Rob. If you open that door, Pablo will come out of the shadows." She clutched his arm.

"I'm not so sure about that, Libby. Look at her face. She's been beaten." His finger twitched on the trigger of his gun as Teresa rapped on the window and uttered a garbled plea.

"What about the baby?" He couldn't take it anymore and turned the dead bolt. "If Pablo's out there and makes a move, he's a dead man. Stand back, Libby."

He yanked open the door and grabbed Teresa's arm through the narrow space. "Get inside."

Teresa tripped across the threshold, and Libby steadied her.

Then through swollen and bloodied lips, Teresa said in Spanish, "You have to get away. He was sent here to kill you."

Chapter Thirteen

Libby wrapped one arm around Teresa and held on to the baby with the other while Rob secured the front door.

He whipped around, still clutching his gun, and Teresa whimpered. "Is he out there? Does he know you're here?"

Teresa's eyes took up her entire face, which had blanched.

Scowling at Rob, Libby took Teresa's arm and led her to the couch. She could extend sympathy to someone in worse condition than she was. She spoke to Teresa in Spanish. "Rob's not going to hurt you. Where's Pablo?"

Teresa explained that Pablo had put her and the baby on a bus back to Mexico, but she'd gotten off two stops later and returned here.

"To warn Libby? What do you know about Libby? Who's Pablo? Who sent him to kill Libby?"

Libby held up a hand to Rob. "One question

at a time, Rob. You're confusing her... And it doesn't help that your Spanish is atrocious and you're waving a gun around."

Rob shoved the gun in his waist in the back and crouched by the window.

Libby sat next to Teresa and stroked the baby's cheek. She spoke to her in Spanish. "Pablo didn't hurt the baby, did he?"

"No. He wouldn't hurt the baby. She's his daughter, and his name isn't Pablo Bustamante."

Libby nodded but pressed her lips together. He'd hurt his wife but not his daughter? How long would that last? "Why did he hurt you?"

"He said I didn't do enough to make you think Luisa was yours."

"I'm sorry, Teresa. If I thought he was going to harm you, I would've done a better job of playing along."

"No, no. He would've hurt you."

Rob perched on the arm of the chair across from them and asked, "Is she Libby James?"

"Yes." Teresa touched Libby's hand. "You don't remember? You're Libby James, the artist."

"I own a gallery in Rocky Point?"

"Yes."

"Why is Pablo, or whatever his name is, trying to kill me? Why did those other men try to kill me? Are they doing this for El Gringo Viejo?"

"No!" Teresa clutched the baby to her chest so hard, Luisa squeaked. "I don't know anything about El Gringo Viejo."

"But he's in Rocky Point." Rob hunched forward, his hands on his knees.

"I don't know. I don't know anything." Teresa whipped her head back and forth, and the baby whined.

"Your lip is bleeding." Libby touched her own lip. "Rob, can you please bring Teresa a towel and some ice? Water and ibuprofen would be good, too."

Rob stood up and cranked his head as he walked to the kitchen. "Ask her what she's doing here if she's not going to give up Pablo or El Gringo Viejo and can't tell you anything you don't already know."

Libby shook her head and drew a finger across her throat. Seeing the gesture, Teresa started up from her seat on the couch.

"Don't worry. Nothing's going to happen to you here. Rob will protect you."

Teresa dropped back to the cushion and repositioned the baby in her arms. "I'm sorry. I can't tell you anything more about yourself. I know your name is Libby James and you're an artist who lives in Rocky Point. You crossed the cartels in some way, but I don't know how. You left Punto Peñasco in a big hurry, and they went after you. They tried to kill you but failed, so they sent…my husband after you. He brought me and the baby to make you think she was yours."

Rob came back with a wet paper towel, a glass of water and two ibuprofens cupped in his palm. "Why are you here? Why didn't you stay on the bus back to Mexico?"

Teresa's dark eyes glistened with tears. "I'm afraid he'll kill me one day. I—I have relatives in Texas. I want to go there, leave…him. You helped Libby. Maybe you'll help me, too."

"Here, let me have the baby. Take the pills and press that paper towel against your lip." Libby held out her arms for the sleepy baby and cuddled her on her lap.

Rob gave Teresa the makeshift first-aid supplies and jabbed his thumb into his chest. "What am I now, the savior of displaced women?"

Libby cocked her head at him and winked. "Maybe we just know a safe harbor when we see one."

"She does know I'm Border Patrol, doesn't she?"

"I don't think so, Rob, and you're not telling her. Let her go to her relatives. She's trying to help me, and we should help her."

"*Is* she trying to help you?"

"What does that mean?" Libby glanced at Teresa, but she and Rob were speaking too fast for her to follow the conversation.

"Ask Teresa how she knew my house. How do we know Pablo isn't out there right now waiting for us?"

Libby asked Teresa and she admitted that Pablo already knew that Libby was staying with Rob and knew Rob's house. They'd driven past the house earlier. Pablo had asked her to write down the address and that was how she knew how to get back here.

"She's gonna have to give us more, Libby. If we're going to help her, keep quiet about her presence in the country and send her on her way, she has to give us more than your name and the fact that bad guys are after you. We know all that. We figured it out on our own."

Libby took a deep breath. How did you strong-arm a terrorized woman with a baby? "We want to help you, Teresa. We will help you and Luisa get to your relatives, but I have no memory and that puts me in grave danger. If there's anything else you can tell me—what the other men look like who are after me, why they're after me or even if there's someone I can call in Rocky Point for help, someone who knows me."

Libby slid a quick glance at Rob. Had he understood that last part? It's not that she thought she had a husband who could come to the rescue, but maybe she had someone who could fill her in on the details of her life.

Teresa stopped dabbing her lip, her gaze darting from Libby to Rob. She understood the implications of the questions. "I don't live in Punto Peñasco. I don't know you. I overheard my husband's conversations, and they want to stop you before you remember everything that happened. I don't know what that is. He never spoke of it in front of me. I do know when you left Punto Peñasco, you were coming here to Paradiso."

"Rob?" Libby crossed her hands over her chest. "Did you get that?"

Rob looked up from his phone. "Don't rub it in. You two are speaking too fast for me. What did she say?"

"She said she overheard a few of her husband's conversations, and from what she can gather, Paradiso was my destination when I left Mexico."

Rob shoved his phone in his back pocket. "That's weird. Why would you be headed here? It must be because of our Border Patrol office. We're the closest one to the border."

"How would I know that? Average, everyday people minding their own business do not generally know where their nearest Border Patrol office is—especially people living in Mexico."

"Ask her if she heard anything else, and let me have the baby." Rob crouched in front of her.

"Why?" Libby pushed a finger into Rob's chest. "You're not going to imply that you're going to take Luisa if her mother doesn't cooperate, are you?"

His dark eyebrows collided over his nose. "Never even occurred to me. It's great that you can't trust the only person you *can* trust."

"You are in law enforcement, Rob, and sometimes—" she shrugged "—you show that hard edge. I know you want to do your job, and I know you want to help me."

"Yes and yes, but not at the expense of a mother and her child. Ask her." He tilted his head toward Teresa on the couch. "She's beginning to think we're plotting against her."

Libby handed off Luisa, who'd begun fussing, to Rob, and she moved closer to Teresa. "That's helpful that you told me I was originally headed to Paradiso. Can you tell me anything else? Do you know why I was coming to Paradiso?"

"I don't know that—sorry." Teresa twisted the wet paper towel in her fingers. "I-is he going to help me?"

"Yes, we're going to help you." Libby put her

hand over Teresa's. "You need money to get on a bus to Texas?"

"Yes, El Paso."

"Did you get that?" Libby twisted her head around to Rob, who was bouncing a giggling Luisa in his arms.

"She wants to go to El Paso."

"Muy bueno." Libby winked at Teresa. "Can we do that?"

"She's gotta get a ride up to Tucson." Rob pinched the baby's chin. "Don't look at me like that, Libby."

She widened her eyes and fluttered her eyelashes. "Like what?"

"Like I'm the last hope for mankind."

"You are, or at least for displaced women. Can you take Teresa to Tucson tomorrow morning? Or—" she grimaced "—I guess that would be this morning."

"*We* can take her. I'm not leaving you here on your own, and this little one—" he held Luisa up in the air and jiggled her "—needs a car seat."

"Where are we going to get a car seat at this time of the morning?"

"I can borrow one from my buddy. He and his fiancée are adopting a baby, and even though the adoption isn't final yet, they do have a car seat for visits."

Libby turned and translated their conversation, or most of it, to Teresa, the crease finally disappearing between the other woman's eyes.

Rob handed the baby back to Teresa. "You two get ready to go. I'll get the car seat. Do not open that door. If you need it, there's a loaded pistol in my nightstand drawer."

While Rob went to his friend's place and made up some excuse about why he needed a car seat at five in the morning, Libby kept watch at the window with her hand curled around the handle of Rob's gun and watched Teresa feed and change the baby.

Nothing stirred outside until Rob pulled his truck into the driveway.

He used his key to get into the house, as he told her not to open the door for anyone—even him. He burst through the front door, rubbing his hands together. "All quiet here?"

"Everything's fine, and Teresa and Luisa are ready to go." Libby set the heavy weapon down on the table by the front door. "Did you have to do much explaining to get the car seat?"

"Luckily, my friend was home alone. His wife, who would be the one asking all the questions, had already left for the academy."

"Oh, she's the one who's going to be a cop." Libby wrinkled her nose.

"Yeah. My buddy's a lot more laid-back than

she is, so when I told him I had a friend staying with me who needed to borrow a car seat for the morning, he handed it over with no more questions asked." Rob waved his hand behind him. "He's the one who owns all the pecan groves in town and has half ownership of the processing plant. The dude has no worries."

"Must be nice." Libby grabbed her purse and turned to Teresa. *"Estás lista?"*

Teresa nodded and answered in English, "Ready."

As they walked out to the truck, Rob led the way and called over his shoulder. "My friend Nash told me if the baby is under one year old, the car seat faces the back. He helped me put it in. I never realized Nash knew so much about babies."

Libby said, "You're not so bad yourself in that department. I saw how you entertained Luisa. You did good."

"I have plenty of nieces and nephews—some with no fathers around. I learned by doing." He held the back door open for Teresa, who ducked in the truck to secure her daughter in the car seat.

Libby patted Teresa's shoulder. "You can sit in the back with Luisa. You'll be fine now. Does your husband know you have family in El Paso?"

Teresa shook her head.

Rob eyed his rearview mirror. "I'd stop for coffee, but I think it's best we get on the road."

Libby lowered her voice and touched Rob's thigh. "Do you think Pablo might be following us?"

"Don't know, but he's not going to follow us to Tucson, not if I can help it."

Both Teresa and Luisa fell asleep in the back seat, but Libby's nerves wouldn't allow her to doze off. She flicked her gaze to the side mirror almost as many times as Rob glanced at the rearview, her only conversation an occasional "See anything?"

As far as she knew, which wasn't much, she'd never heard of Paradiso before, had never been here, didn't know anyone here. Why would she be on her way to Paradiso?

If she had family here, wouldn't they have seen and recognized her by now? Maybe not. Paradiso was small, but as Rob had pointed out, it had grown with the pecan processing plant. She doubted she'd seen every person who lived in Paradiso.

The only person she wanted to see in Paradiso now was sitting right beside her. If Rob weren't so honorable, they could've made love last night. Maybe she just wanted him because she needed someone to feel close to, someone to fill all the emptiness inside her.

Maybe he was right. Even if she found out she didn't have a significant other in her real life, once she discovered that life she might feel completely different about him. Did that even matter? He didn't want to be hurt. She understood that. Despite his background, despite his buffed-up physique, Rob Valdez was a sensitive guy.

Once he fell for someone, he'd fall hard and never want to let go. Knowing that about him made her ache to be possessed by him, body and soul. You'd know who you were if you were loved by someone like Rob.

"We're just a few miles out. I'm going to take her directly to the bus depot downtown. She can get something to eat there." He flicked a finger at the rearview mirror. "We weren't followed. I know that for a fact."

"Good. He probably thinks she's on her way back to Mexico, still under his thumb. Even though she didn't give us that much info, I'm glad she came to us…you."

"She gave us another piece of the puzzle. We'd wondered where you were going when those two forced you off the road. Now we know you were close to your goal."

"But why?" She scooped her hair back from her face.

"We'll get that piece, too." He cranked his head around to the back seat. "Teresa, *estamos aquí.*"

Libby turned around and patted a sleeping Teresa's knee. *"Estamos aquí."*

Ten minutes later, Rob pulled the truck into a parking space on the street and helped Teresa get Luisa out of the car seat.

Libby grabbed Teresa's small bag and joined them on the sidewalk in front of the bus terminal. Downtown was just waking up, but most businesses were still closed. Nobody on the street watched them or paid them any attention.

She and Rob escorted Teresa and her baby into the terminal. Rob checked the schedules and discovered a bus leaving for El Paso in thirty minutes. He handed Teresa enough cash to buy a ticket and get something to eat along the way.

When they saw the bus off, Rob expelled a long sigh. "At least that's taken care of. I don't know about you, but I need something to eat and I can't wait until we drive back to Paradiso this time."

"Breakfast sounds good. I feel like I haven't eaten in forever, so I'm up for anything."

Rob rolled his shoulders and flexed his fingers on the steering wheel. "I'm thinking we should publish your picture in town now. If someone there is waiting for you, they'll recognize your photo and come forward."

"Someone like Pablo Bustamante." She gripped the edges of the seat. "I don't know enough yet."

"You know you're Libby James, an artist from Rocky Point."

"What if another Pablo comes out of the woodwork?"

"I won't let you go...off with just anyone."

"I'll think about it." She snapped her seat belt. "Where to?"

"There's a place north of downtown called First Watch. Not sure where it is." He handed his phone to her. "Can you look it up?"

She looked up directions to the restaurant and let the GPS lady call them out to Rob. He navigated the streets of Tucson until he pulled into a shopping center.

"Yeah, I remember now, and it looks like it's open for business."

Several minutes later, they took a table by the window and ordered coffee. When it arrived, Libby dumped some cream into her cup.

Taking a sip, she closed her eyes. "Ah, I needed this. We didn't get much sleep last night, did we?"

"You seemed to sleep well." Rob slurped his

own coffee and hid behind the menu the waiter had dropped off.

She tapped his menu. "Why didn't you go to your bedroom?"

"Like I said, you seemed to be sleeping soundly, and I didn't want to wake you up." He peered at her over the top of the menu. "I think I'm going to have one of these skillets."

"I don't think I would've woken up if you'd slipped out. You must've been uncomfortable sitting up all night."

"I kinda slumped over. It wasn't bad." He ran a finger down her menu. "They have some healthy stuff—oatmeal, yogurt and granola."

She raised her eyebrows. "Slumping over was comfortable?"

"All right." He snapped his menu down on the table. "I wanted to stay there and hold you all night long. Is that what you want to hear?"

"That's exactly what I wanted to hear." She smiled as she buried her chin in her hand and studied the menu. "Since you rejected me, flat out."

"Libby, you have no memory. Someone has to be thinking clearly for both of us."

The waiter's eyes popped open as he approached the table. "Y-you ready to order?"

Libby took Rob's advice and ordered the yogurt, granola, fruit bowl. When the waiter walked away, she hunched forward. "Wanting to be with you is the clearest thought I've had since climbing out of that wreck."

"What happens when you remember your husband? You'd feel guilty. I'd feel…guilty." He gulped down some coffee, obviously burning his tongue, as he grabbed his water next.

"Rob—" she smoothed two fingers along the inside of his wrist, tracing the line of his veins "—Libby James doesn't have a husband. If she did, why wasn't he in the car with her… with me? Think about it. I witnessed something, probably a murder, and I fled. Wouldn't I go to my husband first?"

"Maybe your husband's in Paradiso." He swirled his coffee with one hand, leaving the other in her possession. "Did you ever think of that? You were running to him."

She sat back in her seat, pulling her purse over her head and setting it beside her. "That never occurred to me—and that's further proof he doesn't exist."

"Really." Rob folded his arms in that way he had that dared her to prove him wrong.

"The fact that it never crossed my mind proves that there is no husband. I think if I'm going to remember anything in a hypnotic state, it would be a husband, someone I loved and wanted to get to."

"Not necessarily. You remembered the incident that fueled your flight from Rocky Point first. That makes sense."

"Rob—" she curled her fingers around his wrist "—I can't ever imagine forgetting you, forgetting your face. Ever."

His dark eyes glittered, and she knew he felt the heat between them.

"California skillet." The waiter set Rob's plate on the table and slid her bowl of health in front of her. "Anything else?"

"My toast." Rob tapped her cup. "And more coffee when you get a chance."

Libby whistled and grabbed her spoon. "Saved by the waiter."

"I'm never going to forget you, either, Libby, but I don't want to make any mistakes."

Rob had obviously seen too many people make too many mistakes in his life.

"What if I never remember?"

"Jennifer believes you will. You've already started."

"I can't wait." She dug into her yogurt parfait.

"Once you remember everything, that'll go a long way to keeping you safe."

"Yeah. Can't wait for that, either."

While they ate, they tried to steer clear of her problems and his feelings. She pried into his family life a little more, and as that conversation was completely one-sided, she learned a lot about Rob Valdez—and liked him even more because of it.

After downing her second cup of coffee, she whipped the napkin from her lap. “I’m going to use the ladies’ room before we hit the road back to Paradiso.”

“I’ll take care of the check.”

Libby wove through the tables toward the restrooms near the entrance. She tried the door on one, which was locked, and shuffled to the other unisex bathroom as someone came up on her heels.

The handle turned, and as she pushed open the door, the man on her tail shoved her inside the bathroom, crowding inside behind her.

Her heart slammed against her rib cage. Spinning around, she placed her hands against his solid chest and opened her mouth to scream. It was then she felt the barrel of a gun jabbing her gut.

Chapter Fourteen

Rob glanced at the time on his cell phone. A flare of concern fluttered in his gut. Had Libby passed out or something?

He downed the rest of his water and Libby's and made his way to the front of the restaurant. He turned the corner that led to the small hallway where the restrooms were located and almost bumped into a woman coming through one of the two doors.

He caught the door before it closed and peeked inside, but these were single, unisex bathrooms and this one was empty. Sidestepping to the next one, he tried the handle. It resisted.

He knocked. "Libby? You still in there?"

A man's voice answered. "Still in here. Not Libby."

Rob's pulse jumped, and his head jerked to take in the exit door to the side parking lot. Had she gone out that way to wait by the truck?

He took one step toward the door and tripped to a stop. Pivoting back toward the occupied bathroom, he banged his fist against the door. “Libby? Libby, are you in there?”

The door burst open, hitting his foot, and a red-faced man with bunched-up fists charged into the hallway. “What’s your problem, man?”

Rob pushed past the man’s solid form and stumbled into the empty bathroom. He tilted his head back to survey the sealed, frosted window. No way in, no way out of that.

He careened out of the bathroom and grabbed the jacket of the man, who by this time had dismissed him as a nut. “Who was in that bathroom before you?”

The man yanked out of his grasp. “I don’t know what’s wrong with you, dude, but you’d better back off.”

“Sorry.” Rob flipped out his badge. “Border Patrol. I need to know what happened to the woman who was in that bathroom before you.”

“I don’t know if it was the woman or the man who was in the john before me. They were both in the hallway and walking out the exit when I saw them.” He shrugged. “I guess it could’ve been the girl in there before me.”

“Was she wearing jeans and a green top? Long light brown hair?”

“I don’t know what she was wearing. Yeah,

probably jeans, but she had a rockin' body and it looked like her guy appreciated it, 'cause they were walking real close and he had his arm right around her."

Rob turned and ran for the door, every muscle in his body screaming. He shoved through the exit and rushed into the parking lot, his head cranking back and forth.

"Libby! Libby!"

"Rob! Ro..."

When Libby's cry reached his ears, adrenaline coursed through his body and he charged toward the sound. A shuffling, scraping noise got louder as he made his way to the edge of the parking lot.

Hot rage thumped through his veins when he saw Libby struggling against a man with a shaved head, trying to cram her into the driver's seat of a beat-up white sedan, a Wildcats sticker on the back.

Libby was hanging on to the door, her feet planted in the asphalt while the man had one arm hooked around her waist and a hand on her back—a hand holding a gun.

As the man started to raise the gun, Rob stormed at him, pointing his own weapon at his critical mass. "Stop or I'll take you down right now."

Rob held his breath while the man dropped

his arm from Libby's waist. If he pulled Libby in front of him to use as a hostage, Rob would take the shot…a head shot.

Rob growled. "Don't even think about it."

The man released his gun and held up his hands. "Don't make a scene. There are some people coming this way, although they haven't noticed yet what's happening."

"Yeah, we wouldn't want to make a scene while you're abducting my…this woman." Rob's lip curled. What was he, some kind of gentleman kidnapper?

"I know it looks bad, but it's not." The man ran a hand over his shaved head.

Libby kicked the guy in the shin and ran to Rob. "He grabbed me in the bathroom and forced me out here at gunpoint, but when he tried to get me into the car, I resisted. I told him he'd have to shoot me first…and he didn't. Why didn't you shoot me?"

"My name is Troy. I don't want to hurt you, Libby."

"How do you know her name?" Rob's arm curled around Libby's waist, and her body practically vibrated against his.

Troy licked his lips. "I contacted her in Rocky Point. I'm the one she was on her way to meet in Paradiso. I swear to you. I have texts and everything."

Libby's frame had stiffened. "Are you going to tell me you're my husband, and I was coming to you for help? All you want to do now is take me back to Rocky Point and resume our happy life?"

Rob ground his teeth together, his muscles aching, his head throbbing.

Troy turned his head to the side and spit on the ground. "Oh, hell no. I've never met you before in my life, and I've already had two wives. I sure as hell don't want any more…especially ones who kick."

A flood of relief swept through Rob's body so fast, he had to lock his knees to keep upright.

Libby needed him to keep upright. Her body sagged against his. "Wh-what do you want? Who are you, and why did you abduct me at gunpoint?"

Tipping his head at the building behind them, Troy said, "Can we go back into the restaurant and discuss this? My weapon's on the ground, which you can take, and we're gonna start attracting attention. I don't want to explain myself to the police, and I'm guessing you don't, either."

Rob whispered in Libby's ear, "Stay here."

He crept toward Troy and the car, his gun still firmly clutched in his hand. "Kick your weapon toward me and don't try anything, or else one of those ex-wives is going to collect on your life insurance policy."

"That ain't gonna happen. My daughter gets it all." He nudged the weapon toward Rob with his toe. "Take it."

Without removing his eyes from Troy, Rob stooped to snatch up the gun. Then he approached the man, turned him around and shoved him against the car. A pat-down didn't reveal any more weapons.

"Start walking back to the restaurant, and remember..."

"Yeah, I know. My daughter's gonna collect that life insurance." He trudged past Rob, made a wide berth around Libby and plodded toward the restaurant.

If the hostess recognized any of them, she didn't let on, waving them to a booth in the corner. Rob slid in first, letting Libby have the outside in case something went down and she had to make a quick getaway. He motioned Troy to the other side.

As Troy plopped down on the seat, Rob said, "I've got my gun pointed at you. One move and your daughter's going to be an only child."

Troy's eyes widened for a second and then he chuckled. "You're not so bad for a lawman, Valdez."

Rob's eye twitched. "How do you know me,

and how'd you find us here? Nobody followed us from Paradiso. I'd bet my life on it."

"I didn't have to follow you." Troy laced his fingers together and cracked his knuckles. "I put a GPS tracker on your truck."

"Damn." Rob smacked the table with his open hand, and the silverware jumped.

A waitress scurried over. "What would you like?"

"Coffee all around." Rob swept his finger in a circle to encompass the table and then turned over his coffee cup.

Libby said, "Make mine a hot tea, herbal if you have it."

"Chamomile okay?" The waitress filled Rob's and Troy's cups to the brim.

"Perfect."

Rob pinned Troy with a stare. "When did you do that?"

"I'm not giving away all my tricks, lawman." Troy formed his fingers into a gun and pointed at Rob.

"Stop with the quips, Troy, and tell us what you want with Libby."

"Well, I wanted information." Troy rubbed the graying stubble on his chin with his knuckles. "Libby James was supposed to meet me in Paradiso to give me some information, but it doesn't look like that's gonna happen. I figured out soon enough when I saw you in town that you had either changed your mind or had gotten a better deal. You didn't show up at our meeting place, and when I walked straight at you in the street wearing my San Francisco Giants baseball cap and flashing a peace sign, you didn't even blink. That's when I started thinking you didn't remember a thing."

"Oh, God." Libby squeezed her eyes closed and wrinkled her nose. "That was you. I remember now."

"Yeah, I wish you remembered more than that."

"Wait. This is all very clever, but why did you try to take Libby at gunpoint?" Rob drilled his finger into the table in front of Troy.

"You wouldn't have believed me if I'd come up to you and explained who I was." Troy snorted. "I saw what happened to the last guy who tried that."

"Pablo Bustamante." Libby crossed her arms on the table, rubbing at the gooseflesh on her skin. "What do you know about him?"

"Nada. Just that he works for the bad guys, and his name ain't Pablo Bustamante. I figured he was coming on like a husband and was using that baby as a prop. Am I right?" Troy dropped his chin to his chest and raised his brows to his bald head.

"You seem to be right about an awful lot." Libby drew back as the waitress placed her tea in front of her.

"Thanks." She smiled at the waitress and then turned her attention back to Troy. "Who are you, and what information did you hope to get from me?"

"You two haven't figured it out yet based on my slick moves?"

Rob grunted. "You're a PI."

"Bingo, lawman." Troy slurped up his coffee and then dumped some sugar into the cup.

"A private investigator?" Libby ripped open her tea bag and swung it around her finger, pointing at Troy. "Investigating what?"

"I'm investigating El Gringo Viejo. He's a..."

Rob sliced his hand through the air. "We know what he is."

"I figured you did, Valdez, but what about her? I mean, I know she knew about him before she lost her marbles, but does she know about him now?" He shook his head and folded his hands around his coffee cup. "Damn, this is getting confusing."

"I know what he is...now. The first time I heard his moniker was from the lips of two men sent here to kill me."

Troy's eyes bugged out. "That's it, then. He is in Rocky Point like I suspected, and you know who he is." Troy grimaced. "It's not surprising they want to kill you. You can't identify those guys?"

"That's why she's suspicious of everyone she meets—especially people who abduct her at gunpoint." Rob still had a grip on his own gun beneath the table. Could they trust this guy? If Troy *were* working for the cartels, Libby would be dead by now.

Libby fished her tea bag from her cup and watched the drops fall back into the steaming water. "What info was I supposed to give you about El Gringo Viejo? Did I know the man? Associate with him?"

"You and I weren't even sure this guy you knew *was* El Gringo Viejo, but if those two thugs sent here to murder you mentioned his name, it's a good bet he is."

"I know him?" Libby abandoned her soggy tea bag in the saucer and folded her hands in her lap. "How would I know someone like that?"

"You're an artist. You have some fancy art gallery in town." Troy's eyes narrowed to slits. "The man with the big villa on the outskirts of town likes art. He'd contacted you before I did."

"The big villa on the cliffs overlooking the water." Libby's eyes grew glassy as she stared into her teacup as if hoping to read the tea leaves to her past there.

Troy scooted closer to the table. "You remember that?"

"I've seen a hypnotist."

Rob nudged her foot beneath the table. She must already trust this guy, but he'd rather do a little private investigating of his own first.

"Smart move." Troy snapped his fingers. "You didn't remember anything else?"

"I remembered the art gallery, but Rob and I had already done some sleuthing of our own and we deduced that I was Libby James, an artist and gallery owner in Rocky Point." Libby slid a glance at Rob, and he shook his head.

If Troy noticed the gesture, he didn't react. Rob didn't want Libby telling Troy about the dead body she remembered, or anything else, until he had a chance to check him out.

Rob blew out a breath. "Look, what's your name? Your last name. And why are you investigating El Gringo Viejo? How did you know he was in Rocky Point when the Border Patrol, DEA, FBI and the Federales don't know where he is?"

Troy plunged two fingers into the front pocket of his wrinkled shirt and pulled out two business cards. "One for you, and one for you."

Rob picked up the card Troy had placed in front of him on the table. "Troy Paulsen, private investigator. Oh, look here. You have a license and everything."

"That'll make it easier for you to run me, won't it, lawman? I even have a license to carry that gun you're holding on me."

"You don't have a license to draw that gun on an innocent woman."

"I'm sorry, Libby." Troy spread his spatulate fingers on the Formica. "I needed to talk to you, and I knew you wouldn't remember me and our meeting. I was never going to hurt you. I was afraid to approach you in Paradiso with the cartel watching your every move."

"Don't remind me." Libby put her hand to her throat.

"Maybe you need to adopt some better business practices, Paulsen." Rob flicked the corner of the card. "You still didn't answer me. Why are you nosing around El Gringo Viejo, and how'd you get this far?"

"PIs aren't under the same rules and constraints as law enforcement. We can get information in ways you can't and from people who wouldn't give you the time of day. I know people in low places, lawman, unlike you."

"You have no idea." Rob twisted his lips. "Who hired you? Because I know you're not tracking down a cartel supplier out of the goodness of your heart. Is it one of the cartels? If it is, this stops here and now. Libby's not going to be involved with that business."

"No, no, nothing like that. I was working for Adam Hart."

Rob bared his teeth. "That's a lie. Adam Hart is dead, and I know the person who killed him."

"I said I *was* working for Adam Hart. I know he's dead, but it's not because he was looking for El Gringo Viejo."

"Not directly." Rob waved off the waitress hovering with the coffeepot. "Why are you still on the job if your client is dead? Hoping to cash in big if you bring EGV down?"

"Funny you should call him EGV. That's what she calls him."

Rob swallowed. "Who?"

"My new client, the person who hired me—Adam Hart's sister, April Hart, or I guess she's April Archer now. She hired me."

Chapter Fifteen

Libby gasped as Rob's stomach sank.

She dug her elbows into the table and propped her chin in one hand, as she leaned toward Troy. "April hired you to find EGV because she thinks he's her father."

"Wow. How do you know all that? Oh, yeah." Troy smacked his forehead. "She's married to a Border Patrol agent herself. You obviously know April, and you know what she believes."

"Does she know about this?" Rob wagged his finger back and forth between Libby and Troy. "Does she know you came to Paradiso to meet someone from Rocky Point who could ID EGV?"

"She doesn't know nothin'. I don't operate that way. Her brother didn't much like it, but I play it close to the vest. I don't give my clients nothin' until I can bring them results. April?" Troy dusted his hands together. "She doesn't even know what I look like. I contacted her after her brother died, told her what was going on and asked her if she wanted me to continue the investigation. She gave me the green light and transfers money to me when I send her my receipts and accounting every month."

"Sweet deal…for you."

"Hey, man. I get results." Troy drilled his knuckle into the table with every word. "I got the heads-up that EGV was near Rocky Point. I went there for a vacation, put out some feelers and discovered this rich dude had a compound on the coast—electric fences, guards, dogs, the whole nine yards. I also found out he was an art lover. Then it got a little hot, and I had to leave, but not before I discovered the guy's interest in local art. So, I contacted Libby James."

Rob's hand curled into a fist. "And put her in danger."

"I didn't twist your arm, Libby. When I told you what I suspected, you were more than eager to help." Troy skimmed a hand over his head. "I don't know the details, but it seems like you had a particular reason to bring down this guy if he was involved with the cartels. You have no love for the cartels, Libby. You made that clear."

A crease formed between Libby's eyebrows. "Did you get the impression it was personal with me? Some hatred beyond what any decent person would feel for the cartels?"

"Oh, yeah." Troy drummed his fingers on the table. "Don't ask me, though, 'cause I don't know, and now I guess neither do you. What I don't get?"

"Yeah?" Libby met his gaze, and Rob placed a hand on her thigh beneath the table.

"How did EGV know you were on to him, and why did you have those goons on your tail on your way up here? This was supposed to be an informational meeting. You told me you had something to show me. Next thing I know, you blow off the meeting, don't acknowledge me in the street and Paradiso is thick with cartel members looking to kill you."

Libby's hand jerked and her tea sloshed over the edge of her cup.

"Sorry." Troy patted her arm with a clumsy hand. "I suppose you don't have your phone, do you? I got the impression what you had to show me was on your phone, but you didn't want to send it to me."

"I'm assuming it burned up in the car along with my purse, my ID, my suitcase, my life."

Rob asked, "What about your phone? You said in the parking lot you had text messages between you and Libby for proof. I'd like to see those messages, see what she texted you before the accident."

"I have it..." Troy dug in his pocket and withdrew a phone with a pink sparkly case. "Damn, I don't have that particular phone on me. I have a lot of burner phones, and I swap them out just in case."

"Right." Rob snatched up Troy's phone from the table. "Passcode?"

Troy rattled it off, and Rob accessed his phone. He scrolled through enough text messages to see that Troy did have clients, and he had Libby's number saved. He called the number just for the heck of it. It rang and rang and rang.

"Libby's phone was probably destroyed in the car fire."

"I know that now. You don't think I've been trying it?" Troy slumped in his seat. "I guess it's back to the drawing board unless you get your memory back and can tell me what you had."

"Back to the drawing board for you. Libby's out of it."

"Lawman, she ain't gonna be out of it until she starts remembering. There are more Pablos out there, and they have orders to make sure Libby's gone before that happens."

LIBBY SAT IN Rob's truck, pressing her fingers to her temples on both sides of her throbbing head. "What do you think?"

"I think Troy Paulsen is a blowhard, and just listening to him tired me out."

"Do you believe him?" Rob must've believed some part of that story because he gave Troy's weapon back to him. "Because I believe him."

"I don't know why he'd lie about working for April Archer. That sounds like something her brother would get up to, and maybe she figured she'd go along with it to see if Paulsen could come up with something."

"Why do you think April didn't mention it to us when she came over? I realize she didn't know I had come across the border to meet with Paulsen, but El Gringo Viejo came up in the conversation and she even admitted that she suspected he was her father."

"I can give you one reason." Rob wiped his brow and started the engine. "Her husband. I'd bet my last dollar Clay doesn't know a damned thing about this investigation, and he wouldn't be happy about it if he did. April wasn't about to tell me."

He backed out of the parking space and pulled out of the lot.

"Why didn't you want me to tell him about the dead body from my memory?"

"You were spilling enough. No need to give him everything. I'm going to run him. If he checks out as legit, maybe we can schedule another meeting with him and you can tell him about the dead man. He might know who he is."

"Why would I have it in for the cartels?" Libby shoved her hands beneath her thighs to keep them from trembling.

"Why wouldn't you? They're a law unto themselves down there. They wreak havoc and pain up here. I've got it in for them. I would even if it weren't my job."

"Troy said I had a personal issue with the cartels." Libby gnawed at her bottom lip. "What if that dead body is someone I know? Someone I love?"

Rob's knuckles blanched as he seemed to tighten his hold on the steering wheel. "Troy made it sound like you had an issue with the cartels from before and that's why you didn't hesitate to help him. Don't you think you fled *because* of the dead body on the lawn?"

"I don't mean a husband or boyfriend." She trailed her fingertips along Rob's tensed forearm. "I think Troy made it clear I didn't have a significant other in the picture."

"Did he?" Rob dropped one hand from the steering wheel to his thigh. "He said you didn't have a husband."

"Okay, forget I said that." She kicked off her sandals and wedged her feet on the dashboard.

"A loved one could be anyone, not just romantic love."

"Let me check out Troy, and if he's on the up-and-up, tell him about the dead body. Maybe he has some ideas. If his intel down there was any good, he should have an idea about who's in that complex with EGV."

"We should probably tell April we met her PI."

"Not a good idea. It doesn't sound like Troy was going to make himself known to her, so it's none of our business."

Libby's jaw fell open. "None of our business? We could put our heads together on this, and we could hand EGV to the FBI or the DEA. Isn't that important to you?"

"Keeping you safe is more important to me than catching EGV."

She stared at his profile, her mouth in danger of dropping open again. "You're kidding."

"Why would you think that? Haven't I upended my entire life since the day I picked you up?" He tapped the clock on the dashboard. "In fact, I'm going to be late for work."

"Um, you didn't seem that interested last night."

"That was sex. Wanting to protect you is something else, and turning you down, while it wasn't easy, is another way to protect you."

"That's nice to hear, Rob, but it's as much about protecting you."

"Me?" He jabbed a finger in his chest. "I know who I am. I know I'm not married or attached or even dating."

"Which means you're free and clear..." She whipped her head around. "You're not even dating?"

"Went on a few online dates in Tucson, but I've been busy. Then I bought my house. Next, I want to get a dog."

"Priorities." She raised her eyes to the roof of the truck. "What I was saying is that you're free and clear to fall for someone...fall for me. And if that happens and I turn out to have a husband and four children, where would you be? I know you're protecting yourself, protecting your heart, and I don't blame you, but, damn, we've got a thing here."

The corner of his mouth twitched. "Does having no memory give you free rein to say whatever comes into your head?"

"Pretty much." She punched his rock-solid bicep. "Do you deny we have some heat between us?"

Idling at the stop sign, Rob threw the truck into Park, leaned over the console and pressed his soft lips against hers. Her mouth opened, and he slid a hand into her hair and deepened the kiss.

Someone honked behind them, and they sprang apart.

Rob pulled away from the stop sign, the truck lurching as much as her heart, and touched his fingers to his mouth. “I do not deny any heat. In fact, my lips are on fire.”

She traced her own tingling lips with the tip of her finger and sighed. “If we can generate that much passion with a quick kiss at a stop sign in a truck with our seat belts on, why the hell are we wasting time?”

Rob aimed his truck toward the on-ramp and punched the accelerator as he merged onto the freeway. “I’ve been through that before, Libby. I dated someone a few years ago who lied about her marital status. I’m just not doing that again. It was…messy.”

She raised her eyebrows at him. “This wouldn’t be like that, Rob. I wouldn’t lie to you. I’d never lie to you.”

“You’re not in a position to know whether or not you’d be lying, and that’s even…messier.”

She puckered her lips, still feeling the stamp of his kiss on her mouth. How could something so messy feel so right?

They spent the rest of the ride to Tucson avoiding conversation about their feelings—and that kiss. They made good time, and Rob made a U-turn to drop her off in front of Rosita’s.

As she reached for the door, he grabbed her arm. "Be careful. Don't go anywhere by yourself, including the restrooms. Use the ladies' room when it's crowded, during the lunch rush."

"I'll be fine. Are you going to look into Troy Paulsen's background?"

"I am, and there's something else he said that got me thinking."

"He said a lot that got me thinking. What did you pick up?"

"Your phone."

"Yeah, I'm pretty sure that burned up in the wreck. It wasn't on me and I didn't see anything in the husk of that car. That's why you didn't even get through to the voice mail when you called it."

"I didn't see anything, either, but Paulsen mentioned you'd been texting him. I'd like to get your phone records and take a look at your texts, if we can get them. Those could tell us a lot. I wish Paulsen would've had the phone he used with you. Those texts could've told us something."

Libby's heart skipped a beat. "Well, you have his card. You know, I never even thought about that. Just because the phone is destroyed doesn't mean the phone's records disappear."

"Exactly." Rob rubbed his chin. "I may not be able to get those records right away, but they'll definitely shed some light on your thoughts and actions before you hit the road to Paradiso."

"See? Troy was good for something." She kissed her fingers and pressed them against Rob's cheek. "Too messy?"

He slapped his hand against his face where she'd placed her fingers. "Just right."

Libby scrambled from the truck and got to work as soon as she entered the restaurant, her mind wandering to Troy's words during her busy shift. Why would a mild-mannered artist agree to infiltrate the compound of a suspected drug broker? Why would she put herself in danger like that unless she had a strong motivation?

Could that dead body be her motivation? Rob was right. If the dead body prompted her flight from Rocky Point, that person couldn't have been her impetus for getting involved with EGV in the first place.

It must've been something…or someone prior to that.

At the end of the lunch rush, Libby stood in the kitchen and ate a quick taco.

Rosie poked her head inside the window. "Rob is here to pick you up. He looks anxious to see you, practically hopping from one foot to the next."

"I didn't even know he was coming to get

me." She called to Sal, "Sal, can you make a burrito for Rob Valdez? Carnitas, I think."

Sal grinned. "I know what Mr. Rob likes."

She wished she did.

Libby smoothed back her hair and traipsed into the dining room, walking in on a few patrons finishing up their lunches. She waved to Rob. "I ordered you a burrito. Did you find out anything about my phone?"

"I did." He pulled her into the nearest chair. "When I called Paulsen, he told me he fired up the phone he'd used with you and read some texts from you that are important."

"What is it?" Libby gripped the edge of the table she'd just cleaned.

"He wouldn't tell me over the phone. He's heading over here, but he doesn't want to be seen with us in case someone's watching you."

Libby glanced over her shoulder at the door, a chill claiming the back of her neck. "What's the plan?"

"He's going to come in here, place an order and leave his phone on a table, opened to the text he wants us to see. That's it. No other communication. All joking aside, the guy's spooked."

"I know how he feels."

Sal brought Rob's burrito to him personally in a paper bag. "Didn't know you were eating in, boss."

"How are the grandkids, Sal?"

"The oldest is up at U of A."

"Already? You need to retire, hombre."

"The wife and I have a little place on the Gulf. Going out there in a few weeks." Sal saluted and returned to the kitchen.

Rob pulled his burrito out of the bag. "I suppose I should pretend to eat this."

"Sal would be very disappointed if you didn't." She grabbed some napkins from the dispenser and shoved them at Rob, her gaze tracking over his shoulder. "Don't look now, but Troy just walked in."

"Keep an eye on him."

"He's ordering." Libby dabbed a napkin on the table. "He has his phone out. He's talking to Rosie."

Rob rolled his eyes. "I don't need a play-by-play."

"You asked." Libby scooted her chair back from the table. "He's walking this way."

Troy strode past their table on the way to the restrooms without a care in the world.

Libby kicked Rob under the table. "He left his phone at the counter."

"Go talk to Rosie and get his phone. Bring it back here." Rob's head swiveled back and forth. "I don't think we have to worry. Anyone left in here is a customer from before, right?"

"Yes, but how do I know one of them isn't spying on me?" She pushed back from the table and hung over the counter. "Hey, Sal, can we get some more salsa?"

She covered Troy's phone with her hand and slid it into her back pocket.

Rosie appeared from the back, carrying a dish of salsa. "The hot stuff."

"Thanks, Rosie." Libby carried the salsa back to the table. Before she sat down, she pulled Troy's phone from her pocket and tapped it.

A set of text messages in alternating gray and blue popped up under the heading of *LJ*, which must be Libby James. She read them aloud to Rob in a low voice.

"'Where are you now?'"

"'Just crossed the border. I should turn off my phone and get rid of it.'"

"'Why?'"

"'I think I'm being followed. Maybe they're tracking my phone.'"

"'Info on the phone?'"

"'Yes, but I have something else to show you.'"

"'You're gonna toss your phone?'"

"'Have a place to drop it off. It's like a desert campsite for RVs. Unofficial. It's not far.'"

"'Go for it. Be careful.'"

The text messages between Troy and LJ

ended, and Libby spun the phone on the table. "That's it. I left the phone at some campsite. How are we ever going to find that?"

Rob had stopped eating his burrito and held it midway between his mouth and the bag on the table. "I know exactly where it is."

"You do?"

Troy came barreling out of the bathroom, rubbing his hands together. "Is my order up?"

"Another few minutes, sir." Rosie greeted another couple coming through the door, and Libby swept the phone off the table. She cupped it between her hands.

"Done with this?" She grabbed the salsa and returned to the counter, making a wide berth around Troy.

She held up the salsa with one hand and slipped the phone back onto the counter with the other. "Here you go, Rosie."

"You hardly touched it, Rob."

"I'm gonna wrap this up and take it home for later, Rosie."

As Libby sauntered back to the table, Rob folded the yellow wax paper around his food and stuffed it in the bag. He glanced up at her. "Ready?"

"Ready for anything."

When she got to the door, she waved to Rosie,

who was handing Troy a bag of food. “Bye, Rosie. See you tomorrow.”

“Day off tomorrow, Jane. We’re closed on Sunday.”

She and Rob slipped out the door and made a beeline for his truck. Troy wouldn’t want to run into them outside.

Once inside the truck, Rob started the engine and took off down the street, back toward his house.

“Are you going to tell me where my phone is?”

“There’s an RV campsite, and I use that term loosely, between Paradiso and the border. It’s unofficial and unregulated. Lots of lowlifes there, so I’m not sure how you knew about it and why you’d leave your phone there.”

“Are we just supposed to bust in there and ask for a phone?”

“If you left it there, you left it with someone. You must know someone there.” He cranked up the AC and wiped his brow. “Believe me, strangers do not just waltz onto this property and ask nicely if they can stash their cell phones. A man was murdered there last month, a baby kidnapped.”

Libby covered her mouth. “Is it safe?”

“Not really, but as much as I’d like to, I can’t barge in there myself. You have to come along and hope someone recognizes you and hands over your phone."

"Almost as important as the phone will be this person who knows me. Finally, someone who knows Libby James."

"But why there?" Rob chewed on the side of his thumb, and Libby slapped his hand.

"Stop that. I'll be okay—as long as I have you by my side. That's one thing Libby James does know."

Rob sped home and changed out of his uniform into a pair of jeans, a dark T-shirt and running shoes.

He pointed to her light-colored capris, filmy blouse and sandals. "You might want to change. It's a dirty, dusty place out there. Did you happen to buy a pair of sneakers when you went shopping the other day?"

"I did." She kicked off her sandals and hooked her fingers around the straps, dangling them at her side. "Why? Am I gonna have to make a run for it?"

"You never know out there."

She changed into clothes appropriate for a quick getaway, and Rob grabbed a backpack on their way out the door. He turned to her when they got to the truck and said, "We're going out past the site of the wreck. Can you handle it?"

"Do you mean am I going to freak out and

have memory flashes that take me back to the crash?" She climbed into the truck. "I hope so."

Thirty minutes later, they passed the crash site without incident. Libby even tried to remember by squeezing her eyes closed and thinking the calming words Jennifer used to put her in a hypnotic state. Libby opened one eye and rolled it toward Rob. "Nothing."

He took her hand and threaded his fingers with hers. "It'll come, and this will all make sense."

"And maybe you and I…?"

"Maybe we will." He squeezed her hand.

She brought their clasped hands to her lips and kissed his knuckles. "It's the only hope I can hold on to right now, Rob."

When Rob turned off the main highway and the truck kicked up dust and dirt on an access road, Libby swallowed. "Where is this place?"

"Where nobody can find them. It's like a commune. People go there to drop out and live off the grid."

"I obviously know someone well enough there to drop off my phone." She ran her hands down the denim covering her thighs. "I hope that person is there today."

The desert undulated with one sandy hill resembling another, and the truck bounced and pitched as the road got rougher.

"Are you sure this is the right way?" Libby

squinted out the windshield, and like a ragtag mirage, a collection of temporary and impromptu houses sprang up in the form of RVs, trailers and cars. "Those came up fast."

"There's a reason they chose this spot. Once someone comes over that rise like we just did, they can see 'em coming."

Libby licked her dry lips. "They're not going to charge us or anything, are they?"

"No." Rob hunched over the steering wheel. "But it looks like they're sending a welcoming committee."

Libby picked out two motorcycles heading their way, a cloud of sand following them. "Do you want your gun?"

"I've got it on me. Don't worry." Rob powered down his window and eased off the gas pedal.

One motorcycle veered right and one veered left, and then they both swung around to come up alongside the truck.

Rob slowed to a crawl and stopped, calling out the window at the rider on his side, "Can we help you boys?"

The biker, a tattoo snaking up his neck, shouted over the sound of his rumbling engine. "What do you want here?"

"We've come to pick up a phone." Rob jerked his thumb to the side toward Libby.

The guy ducked his head and nodded. He circled

his finger in the air and gunned the bike's engine, sending a shower of sand and dust into the truck.

The biker on Libby's side got the message and shot forward, both of them cruising back to the campsite.

Libby coughed and waved a hand in front of her face. "That was easy. I thought we were going to have to take them out for a minute."

"They recognized you." Rob rubbed the back of his hand across his nose. "They've seen you here before and you must be welcome, or they would've tried to stop us."

"That's a good sign, right?"

"Excellent sign. We're in." Rob followed the hazy air in the path of the bikes to the makeshift campsite.

When they arrived, the two watchdogs had already gotten off their motorcycles and were retreating to some dilapidated RV. Rob parked the truck just outside the official entrance to the compound and cut the engine.

"Just walk in there like you own the place, like a boss."

"I've never felt less like a boss." Libby hitched her purse over her shoulder, but this time she waited for Rob to come around and open her door. She had no intention of waltzing into that squalid encampment demanding her phone.

Rob took her arm, even though he couldn't

possibly know her knees were knocking together. He whispered in her ear, "It's okay. We got this."

As they scuffed into the center of the camp, a woman with cropped gray hair and an armful of tattoos floated out to greet them. She put her arms around Libby and said, "I'm glad you're safe, my sweet. I have your phone."

Libby reared back from the woman's embrace, tears stinging her eyes. "You know me?"

The woman's gray brows arched over her eyes. "What does that mean? Of course I know you, Libby. Your mother was one of my dearest friends. What's going on?"

"Ma'am." Rob held out his hand. "My name is Rob Valdez. Libby ran into some trouble north of the border. Some men forced her off the road. Her car crashed and she lost her memory. We've been able to piece together some things, but she has huge holes in her memory—and she's in danger."

The woman's light blue eyes grew larger and larger with every word from Rob's lips. Then she clasped Libby to her breast again and cried out, "I knew I shouldn't have let you go. Do you know you're Libby James?"

"I do." Libby inhaled the scent of this woman—herbs and earth and spice. Comfort. An overwhelming sense of calm seeped into Libby's bones. She knew this woman. "Luna."

Rob's head jerked to the side. "You remember her?"

"That's right, my sweet. I'm Luna." Luna patted Libby's back. "Do you remember me?"

"I—I remember your smell. Your name came to me from your scent."

"They do say smell is the most powerful sense and can evoke all kinds of memories." Luna smoothed her hand over Libby's face. "Were you physically injured?"

"Just a gash on my head. Otherwise, I'm fine."

Luna's gaze darted around the campsite. "Come to my home. We're attracting attention out here, and I don't want anyone knowing our business."

With her arm curled around Libby's waist, Luna led them to her RV, one of the nicest in the collection, a colorful blue-and-white awning fanning out over some chairs and a small pit for a campfire.

Luna patted a canvas chair. "Sit here, Libby. I'm going to try to help you. I don't know why you were on the run from Rocky Point. You wouldn't tell me that, but I can help you with the rest. I can't imagine the fear of having a black hole for a memory."

Libby sank to the chair, crossed one leg over the other and promptly started kicking her leg.

"It's been crazy, made worse because of the danger and made better because of… Rob."

"Call me old-fashioned, but I think everything's better with a partner by your side." Luna winked at Rob and waved him into a chair.

Libby blinked. "And you have a partner. He lives here with you."

"That's right." Luna nodded, a broad smile displaying her white teeth. "Zeke, who's scavenging in the desert right now. I'd say he's pretty unforgettable. See? You're remembering already. It must help to be with people you know. No offense, Rob."

"None taken."

"Luna—" Libby's blood bubbled in her veins "—you mentioned you were friends with my mother. Where is she? Is she in the States? Back in Rocky Point? Is she worried?"

The creases in Luna's lined face softened. "I'm sorry, Libby. Your mother is dead."

Luna's words punched her in the gut, and Libby pressed a fist to her belly. "H-how long ago? What happened?"

"It was just a few months ago." Luna clasped her hands around one knee. "Tandy was murdered, Libby."

Tandy? Rob sucked in a breath and choked out, "Oh, my God. Libby's mother was Tandy Richards?"

Chapter Sixteen

Libby stared at him, her eyes wide in her pale face. "Where have I heard that name before, Rob? I've heard the name."

"I guess I mentioned the name once, or you overheard me." Rob clenched his teeth. Libby didn't have to remember those details, and if she couldn't recall the conversation, he wasn't going to refresh her memory.

Then she wailed and doubled over, her forehead touching her knees. "She was beheaded. My mother was one of the mules who was murdered in the tunnel."

Luna stroked Libby's hair and glared at Rob over the top of Libby's head.

He'd gone from hero to zero with one stupid statement.

Luna murmured, "I'm sure that's just a rumor, Libby. There are all kinds of gruesome tales circulating around the border."

Libby straightened up, sweeping her hands

across her wet cheeks. "No, you don't understand. Rob is a Border Patrol agent. He mentioned something about the two women, the two mules, who were decapitated at the border. He said their names, Tandy Richards and Elena something."

Luna pressed her lips into a straight, thin line. "You're Border Patrol?"

Rob lunged out of his chair and knelt before Libby, wrapping his arms around her waist and burying his face in her lap. "I'm sorry, Libby. I never in a million years would've connected you to Tandy Richards. I should've never mentioned that case to you."

Her fingers slipped into his hair. "My mother was a mule for the cartels?"

Luna said, "Your mother was a troubled woman, Libby, but she loved you and had the biggest heart."

"My father?"

Rob sat back on his heels and held her hands. He'd rather she have a husband in the wings than this.

Luna sighed. "Not in the picture. Your mother moved to Mexico with you when you were a child. She got mixed up with the wrong people."

Libby clenched her hands in her lap. "That's why I agreed to help Troy."

"Who's Troy?" Luna cocked her head, looking like a bird on alert.

"Never mind, Luna. Knowing my mother died at the hands of the cartels, as painful as it is, clears up a lot." Libby reached for Rob and touched his chin. "It's not your fault. This is the fear I have of remembering everything. I must have already grieved for my mother and it's hit me like a sledgehammer all over again."

Luna pressed a hand to her heart. "Please tell me you didn't decide to go after the cartels on your own to avenge Tandy's death."

"Not on my own, anyway. It's complicated, Luna."

Rob stayed crouched by Libby's side, his hand caressing her calf. "Do you have Libby's phone, Luna? We're hoping that's going to tell us even more."

"It's in the RV. I left it turned off, like you asked, Libby. It might need charging." Luna rose to her feet and climbed the two steps to the aluminum door to her home. She banged around inside and then called out through the window. "I'm charging it now. Give it some time."

Libby cupped his face with her hands. "I'm all right. I always felt there was something I didn't want to remember, and it didn't have to do with the dead body."

"If it makes you feel better, Tandy Richards

did not come up on our radar as having any connections to the cartels or any drug dealers."

"She was a user, Libby." Luna picked her way down the steps, holding two cups of steaming liquid, the scent of peppermint wafting through the air. She handed one cup to Libby. "Do you want some tea, Rob? It's jade citrus peppermint. It'll relax Libby."

"I'll pass, thanks." He placed a kiss on the inside of Libby's wrist and backed up to his own chair. "What do you mean she was a user? Drugs or people?"

Luna shrugged as she sipped her tea. "A little of both. I think someone convinced her to carry for the cartels, or maybe she just went along with the other girl to give her some protection. That's something she'd do."

Libby inhaled the smell of her tea before taking a sip. "Were we in touch? Estranged? Did we live together?"

"Drink some more of your tea." Luna poked a stick at the firepit. "Gets a little chillier out here at night than in the city. A fire's nice. Rob, you wanna get one started? My man Zeke set it up before he left today."

Luna tossed a box of matches at him, and Rob caught them with one hand. As he shoved the kindling beneath the logs, Luna's low, soothing voice floated over him.

"Do you remember your mother, Libby? Pretty woman, like you, but she never had your strength. Always got by on her looks, Tandy did, and when those started to fade she panicked a little. Always enjoyed the company and flattery of men. Do you remember, Libby?"

Libby's eyes had drifted closed, as she drank more tea from her cup. "She was small, petite like a fairy, and she had a laugh that bubbled like champagne. I adored her, but as I grew up, I knew she couldn't protect me."

Rob glanced up from his Boy Scout activity, jerking his head toward Luna, who put a gnarled finger to her lips.

Luna's monotone voice continued. "She did secure the gallery for you, though, and a few wealthy investors. Do you remember?"

The smooth skin between Libby's eyebrows puckered. "We argued about it. She got money from her boyfriend, her rich, married boyfriend, and I told her that's the only way she ever got by in life—using men. I didn't want to accept the gallery, but she cried and said it was the only thing she had ever given me. I felt sad. I accepted the gallery."

"And made a success out of it."

"I wanted Mom to stay with me, but I told her she had to get off the drugs and booze. She wouldn't. We were estranged at the end. She wouldn't change, couldn't change." Libby's eyes flew open, and she pinned Rob with her gaze. "She knew that man in the palatial house. Somehow she knew him."

Rob struck a match and lit the kindling in several places with a slightly trembling hand. As the smoke curled up, he looked at Libby through the haze. "Do you remember now? Everything?"

Waving her hand in front of her face to dissipate the smoke, she shook her head. "Not everything. Not clearly. I can picture my mother. I know she talked to me about the man on the cliff and his interest in art. After she was murdered and Troy approached me, I knew I could get into the compound because my mother knew someone there. He sent her to her death, didn't he? El Gringo Viejo?"

"No, not directly, Libby. It was a small-time drug dealer working for the Las Moscas cartel who wanted to strike out on his own. He's the one responsible for your mother's death—and he paid with his own life." Rob stepped back from the crackling fire. "I wonder if EGV knew what happened to your mother. I wonder if you were in danger from the moment you stepped through the gates of his home."

"That's still a blank, Rob. I don't remember

the man at the house. I don't remember the man who died."

"Someone else died?" Luna tossed the dregs of her tea into the fire, which snapped and danced. "You never told me any of this, Libby."

Libby held up her cup. "What's in this tea? I felt like I did when I was under hypnosis at the therapist's office."

"Hypnosis is just a state of deep relaxation. That's all I did." She pinged her fingernail against her cup. "I put you in a state of deep relaxation and gave you a few suggestions."

"It worked."

Luna asked, "Who's El Gringo Viejo?"

"You don't need to know." Rob circled around the fire and squeezed Libby's shoulders. "Are you all right?"

"I'm fine. I feel like the pieces are falling into place for me."

"Your phone is probably sufficiently charged to go through it." He held out his hand toward Luna. "Do you want me to take your cup? Is it okay if I go inside?"

"Take the cup, go inside, don't disturb the cat." She handed him her cup. "The phone's by the sink, not that our place is all that big."

As he turned toward the steps, Libby grabbed his hand and said, "One more thing, Luna. I'm pretty sure I know the answer, but I'm not married, am I? Have any boyfriends lurking around?"

Luna chuckled. "You're one hundred percent single. Your mother was lamenting that fact the last time I saw her."

Rob swooped down and planted a kiss on Libby's mouth. "Thanks for asking."

He tromped up the two steps and yanked open the door to the RV. His nostrils flared at the smell of that tea in here. Luna must burn the stuff, too.

Spotting the charging phone on the small counter next to the stainless-steel sink, Rob took one step and reached for it. He could probably stand in the center of the RV and reach practically everything.

The gray tabby glared at him from his one good eye, and Rob yanked the charger out of the socket along with the phone before the cat got any ideas.

The battery meter in the corner of the display read half-full, so he held his thumb down on the power button. He stepped out of the RV as the phone came to life and tripped on the bottom step when he saw the familiar keypad for the log-in.

He held up the phone. "Good news and bad news. The phone is powered up and working, but you have a passcode."

"Let me have it." Libby snapped her fingers and opened her palm.

He placed the phone in her hand and hovered over her shoulder.

She hesitated for a split second, and then her thumb darted over the keypad and the screen woke up. Cranking her head over her shoulder, she said, "I remembered, or my fingers remembered."

"Bring up your texts."

Luna half rose from her chair. "Should I leave you?"

"Stay, please, Luna." Libby flicked her fingers at the older woman. "I may need your help."

Rob poked at the screen. "There's your conversation with Troy."

"But I don't see anything that adds to that story." She tapped through the messages. "Wait."

Rob leaned forward, squinting at the lit display. "What do you see?"

"Text messages to and from a Charlie." She drummed her fingers against her chin. "Charlie."

Her phone dinged. "Hey, look. It's a text from Troy asking if I retrieved my phone."

Rob said, "You don't need to answer him now."

"Too late. I just responded Yes."

"Check your photos, Libby. You told Troy you'd have something to show him. You left your phone here to protect it when you knew someone was following you. It has to contain the info you were going to show Troy."

She tapped the photo icon. Gasping, she drew back from the phone. "I-it's Charlie. This is Charlie, Rob. The dead man. I took a picture of him before I left."

Rob's heart rate picked up as he made a grab for Libby's phone. Cupping it in his hand, he focused on the silver-haired man sprawled on the grass, blood soaking his shirt. "Charlie? This is the man you knew as Charlie?"

"Yes. He was my mother's friend or boyfriend. I went to sec the man Troy suspected of being April's father about a purchase from the gallery and found Charlie dead on the lawn. That's when I ran."

"Libby, April's father isn't El Gringo Viejo."

"How do you know that? How can you be so sure?"

Rob tapped the photo on the phone. "Because your Charlie is C. J. Hart, and he's April's father."

Chapter Seventeen

"What?" Libby whipped her head around. "How do you know that?"

"I've seen pictures of C. J. Hart. He's still a wanted man. Even though his son may have confessed to murdering his mother, C.J. is still a fugitive. I know what C. J. Hart looks like, and this man is C.J."

"Oh, my God." Libby's hand dropped to her stomach, her fingers clutching the material of April's T-shirt. "I don't know what's worse, telling April her father is El Gringo Viejo and very much alive or telling her that he's Charlie Harper and very much dead."

"The latter—definitely the latter. So, he was living life as Charlie Harper."

Luna stretched her hands to the fire, wiggling her fingers. "Are you telling me Tandy was involved with a man, a wanted fugitive, who was involved with a drug dealer?"

"It seems so, Luna." Libby's lips trembled.

"And he's probably the one who convinced her to go into that tunnel."

Rob slipped the phone back into Libby's hand. "Maybe not. He obviously helped you get onto the compound. He had to know what that would mean."

"It cost him his life. EGV must've found out what he'd done."

"Maybe he wanted his own revenge against him for Tandy's death." Rob placed a hand on top of Libby's head, her silky hair warm from the fire.

"But where's our proof?" She swept her fingertip from one picture on her phone to the next. "Was I just going to show Troy the picture of a dead Charlie? Was it to prove C.J. wasn't EGV? I don't think I ever heard of C. J. Hart."

"Why would EGV send his goons after you if that's all it was?" Rob sank to the RV steps. "Unless he knew the rumor about C. J. Hart being El Gringo Viejo. He may have even encouraged that rumor to keep the heat off of himself."

"There has to be something here, Rob. A picture of him. I must be able to ID him, and that's why he's so worried. That's why he's after me."

"Do you really think that man would allow you to take his picture? After all these years of staying under the radar? But you have seen him. You can identify him, and worse for him?" Rob extended his hands and flexed his fingers. "You're an artist. You don't need a photo of him. Once you remember everything about him, you can draw him."

"That notepad at the house—maybe I've already drawn him, just as I sketched my mother. I drew her as a beautiful fairy, how I wanted to remember her before disappointment and drugs stole her looks."

"I found that notebook." Rob shook his head. "You didn't draw any men, except for me and some faceless devil. Believe me, I looked…for other reasons. Our best move now is to somehow convince EGV that you've regained your memory—all of it. And you've ID'd him to the authorities. They'd have no reason to want to see you dead once you turn that information over to the cops."

"Except revenge." Luna spread her hands. "I'm sorry, but that's the way those guys are."

"The sketch must be somewhere. I probably had it with me in the car on my way to meeting Troy." Libby's heart flip-flopped in her chest. "Rob, I think I know where it is."

"A drawing of El Gringo Viejo?"

"Stupid, stupid me." She banged her fists against the arms of the chair. "It survived the car fire, and I just threw it away."

"What are you talking about? You had a drawing at the crash site?"

She balled up her fists against her eyes. "While I was sitting out there behind the tree waiting for…you, a piece of paper skittered past me. I snatched it up and smoothed it out. It was a drawing of a man—longish hair, glasses… I don't know. I thought it was trash. I never dreamed it came from the car… But it did. It must've been my drawing of EGV. I was bringing it to my meeting with Troy."

"What did you do with it?"

"I crumpled it up and tossed it." She hunched forward, gripping her knees. "It could still be there, Rob. It might be faster than waiting for my memory to return."

Luna coughed. "Not tonight you're not. Sun's already going down."

Rob rubbed his hands together. "Let's go back to Paradiso. We can head out to the crash site tomorrow morning. If we take some of Luna's magical tea with us, maybe we won't need to go out there. Maybe you'll get your memory back and you can draw it again. We can get it, and his name or alias, into the system and let him and his associates know we're on to him. It'll be too late for them then, Libby. They'll leave you alone."

"Except for that revenge thing." Luna pushed

out of her camp chair. “Zeke’s back. I hear his bike.”

Tilting her head, Libby picked up the sound of a high whine in the distance of the still night. “If Rob was joking, I’m not. Can I take some of that tea with me?”

“Of course.” Luna climbed the steps into the RV and returned with a plastic baggie of loose tea leaves just as a motorcycle pulled into the campsite.

The biker cut the engine and rolled his Harley to the RV. An old Native American climbed off the bike, throwing his long gray braid over his shoulder. “Libby’s back.”

Luna planted a kiss on the man’s brown weathered cheek and turned to Libby. “Do you remember Zeke, Libby?”

Libby rose on unsteady legs, unsure what to do. Should she pretend she remembered him? Shake his hand? Hug him?

“Remember me? Have I aged that much in a week?”

“Zeke.” Luna rested her hand on Zeke’s shoulder. “Libby’s had a rough time since she left us. She had an accident and lost her memory.”

“That’s crazy. How’d you make it back to Luna, Libby?”

“It’s a long story, Zeke. I’ll tell you about it later. These two have to get back to Paradiso.”

She thrust the bag of tea at Libby. "Take this. Relax, clear your mind, think."

Zeke stepped forward and wrapped an arm around Libby, squeezing her close. "Be careful out there, Libby. These desert roads at night… Just saw another car veer off the road, not far from here."

Luna's brow wrinkled. "Did you stop, Zeke?"

"There was another car behind him, and it pulled over. Didn't think an old guy like me without a phone would be much help."

"This is Rob Valdez." Luna waved her arm in Rob's direction. "He's Border Patrol… But he's helping Libby."

Zeke shook Rob's hand. "As long as you're helping our Libby, you're okay with me. She's had enough trouble rolling her way lately."

"She knows about Tandy." Luna stood on her tiptoes and kissed Libby's cheek. "Take care and let us know if we can do anything to help. You know, I don't like the direction this camp has been moving—too much riffraff, too many rough types. But those same rough types are not going to let anyone in here who's not on the guest list."

Rob jerked a thumb over his shoulder. "We noticed."

"We're going to hit the road, Luna." Libby rubbed her stinging nose. "Thanks for all your help. I'll be back—when I remember everything."

"When you do, and this man is caught—" her gaze flicked to Rob "—you can go back to your beautiful life. Because you do have a beautiful life waiting for you, Libby."

Zeke escorted them to the truck, and as he shook Rob's hand again, he said, "Watch yourself out there, but I suppose I don't have to warn a BP agent."

Zeke gave Libby another hug and stood at the entrance of the compound, watching them drive off.

Libby patted the baggie. "Maybe I should drink this at my next appointment with Jennifer. I can sort of see how this is going to work."

"How what's going to work?" Rob had started the truck and maneuvered back onto the access road with the truck shaking and rattling with every mile.

"This memory thing." Libby tapped the side of her head. "I thought everything would come back to me in a flash, but it's more like bits and pieces—conversations, scenes, faces, even feelings."

"As if we needed any more proof that the mind is strange and mysterious." He brushed her cheek with his knuckle. "I'm sorry about your mother. I don't care what she was doing—

nobody deserves that. Maybe she was trying to protect Elena, the other woman."

"I'll hold on to that thought." She propped her elbow on the armrest and cupped her chin in her palm. "Now we have to tell April her father is dead."

"But we can also tell her he's not EGV." Rob accelerated when he hit the dark highway, his high beams creating a cone of light on the road.

"He was still involved with him in some way."

"She already knew C.J. was no angel. True, it turned out he didn't murder April's mother, but the reason his son was able to manipulate him into running was because of his association with the drug trade. When will people learn?"

"It must seem like easy money to them. Look at your own family. Is that what drove them? The money?"

"I'm sure that was part of it—power, control… There are a lot of moving pieces."

"But it never got you."

"It never got you, either."

They drove in silence for a while, maybe both of them pondering how they'd escaped the shared curses of their families.

Libby grabbed Rob's hand and kissed the back of it, savoring the feel of his flesh against her lips and the scent of the fire that lingered on his skin. "I'm so glad you found me that night."

"I am, too." His gaze flew back to the road and he jerked the steering wheel. "Whoa. That must be the wreck Zeke mentioned, but it's still there. The car that pulled over didn't call 911?"

She jabbed him in the ribs. "Maybe someone else lost their memory and didn't want to notify authorities."

Rob's truck crawled up the road, and he swung into a gravel turnout. "I'm gonna check it out. Stay in the truck."

Rob dragged his weapon from beneath his seat and holstered it as he got out of the vehicle.

He'd pulled up behind the wrecked car at a crazy angle off the road, so Libby released her seat belt and scooted up in her seat to peer over the dashboard. A feather of fear whispered across the back of her neck as she watched him cautiously approach the damaged vehicle.

He'd left his headlights on to illuminate the scene, and Libby's gaze traveled from Rob to the car—an old white sedan, Wildcats sticker on the back window. Just like Troy's car.

Gasping, she braced her hands against the dashboard. It *was* Troy's car. She grabbed the door handle and scrambled out of the truck, her feet slipping on the gravel below.

She stalked toward Rob, now leaning forward, his face at the window—the shattered window. Her heart pounded, the blood ringing in her ears. "Rob!"

He spun around, his face white against the black backdrop of the desert night. "Stay back, Libby."

Her adrenaline spurred her forward, her feet barely able to keep pace with her intent. She rushed to the car and loomed over Rob's shoulder, gawking at the sight of Troy Paulsen—dead in the front seat, a bullet wound in his head.

Chapter Eighteen

Libby choked behind him, and Rob turned and grabbed her by the shoulders. "You don't need to see this, Libby. Go back to the truck. Hurry."

He looked around the scene, the desert floor cloaked in darkness. They could still be here. They could be anywhere.

He shook Libby's rigid frame. "Wait in the truck. I'm gonna check things out, and then I'm going to call it in. If the highway patrol can't get here fast enough, we're not going to wait. We're getting out of here."

Her head snapped up. "It was them, wasn't it? The same people who are after me, the people trying to protect EGV, killed Troy."

"Probably. That's why you have to get out of here. Duck down and lock the doors. The keys are still in the ignition. If anything happens out here, take off."

"And leave you? I'll mow them over with the truck first."

He landed a kiss on her forehead. "Not if they're shooting at you. Go."

She shuffled her feet and then turned and ran back to the truck.

Troy's door had been left ajar, so Rob nudged it open with his foot. They probably didn't want to make the same mistake they'd made with Libby. They wanted to make sure they killed their target this time.

He leaned into the car across Troy's body and studied the center console. A coffee cup occupied one of the cup holders and some loose change the other. Rob snatched up some receipts and scraps of paper. He didn't want to dismiss anything and possibly ignore any potential evidence.

He eased the door back into position and went around to the passenger side, shading his eyes and glancing back at the truck. No silhouette of Libby in the window, so she'd taken his advice and slumped in the seat.

Using his T-shirt to cover his hand, he opened the passenger door and ducked his head inside the car, his nose wrinkling at the smell of blood and death. He couldn't say he'd gotten accustomed to the smell, but at least he no longer puked like he had the first time he'd seen a headless body at the border. That body had been Libby's mother.

His gut knotted but he continued his search of the car. It wasn't here. They'd taken Troy's phone.

He dug his own phone from his pocket and called 911, the only call he could make out here. "I want to report a single-car accident about a mile and a half north of mile marker nine. The driver is dead."

After making the call, Rob stalked back to the truck and slid behind the wheel. He handed Libby the papers he'd retrieved from Troy's console. "Can you make any sense out of these?"

"Let me see." She hit the dome light button with her knuckle and dropped the slips of paper in her lap. "Did you find out anything?"

"I found out they took Troy's phone."

Libby's hands froze and one of Troy's receipts floated to the floor. "Then they know he texted me, and they saw my response that I picked up my phone. You were right. I should've never answered him."

"If Troy's even the one who texted you. It could've been one of them, testing the waters." He picked up her phone in the cup holder and handed it to her. "What time did you get that text from Troy's phone?"

She grabbed her phone and tapped the display. "At seven thirty."

He glanced at the time glowing on his dashboard. "It's almost nine o'clock now. We've been on the road for about forty-five minutes, which means we left the campsite around eight fifteen."

"It could've been Troy." Libby held out her hand and ticked off each finger. "Troy texts me at seven thirty, gets killed ten minutes later, and then Zeke sees the accident at seven forty and hits the campsite thirty minutes later?"

"He must've been driving awfully fast."

"He was on a motorcycle. He knows the lay of the land."

Rob placed a hand on Libby's bouncing knee. "Who are you trying to convince? It doesn't matter whether they sent the text or not. Even if Troy had sent it, they have his phone and they've seen the text exchange."

She held the phone in her lap. "Should I text him again? Play along like I haven't seen the accident, don't know Troy's dead?"

He didn't like the idea of Libby texting with a bunch of killers. "What would you text?"

"I would text him that the phone contains no information, no pictures, no names, no nothing. That it's useless and I remember nothing."

Rob expelled a ragged breath. "Do it."

Libby held the phone close to her face and tapped the display, reading aloud as she typed. "'Got the phone. Nothing on it. Can't help you. Can't remember.'"

Rob held his breath as he watched the phone

glowing in Libby's hands. When it dinged, he practically jumped out of his seat. "Response?"

"'Okay.'" She snorted. "Just 'okay.' Definitely not Troy Paulsen. I don't think the guy ever gave a one-word response in his life."

"At least your message is out there. They can believe it or not." He cocked his head. "Hear that?"

"Sirens. The first responders are here. What are we going to tell them?" She wedged her phone in the cup holder again.

"That we saw the wreck, determined the driver was dead and called 911." Rob shoved his weapon into its holster. "We don't know him, don't recognize him, didn't see anyone around."

"What about Zeke? Should we tell them Zeke is the one who spotted the wreck and another car in the vicinity?"

"Not without letting Zeke know first." Rob drummed his thumbs on the steering wheel. "In fact, I want to go back to Luna and Zeke's place and question him...and warn him."

"Warn him?" The lights from the emergency vehicles cast a red-and-blue halo around Libby's hair, making it look like fire.

"If the people who killed Troy saw Zeke's bike, noticed anything about him, he could be in trouble. He should at least know what he stumbled on. Luna mentioned she didn't much like the new residents of the camp. Maybe this is their opportunity to move on."

Libby clasped her hands. "I didn't even think about it. Luna and Zeke could be in danger."

"I suppose they don't have a phone, do they?"

"Nope."

"Then we'll have to drive out there when we're done with this." He squeezed her neck, his fingers pressing into her soft skin. "Are you up for that?"

"Of course. I don't want to see them get hurt. Those other bikers there might not provide any protection if they think the cartel will come after them, or if the cartel pays them off." She grabbed the handle of the truck when the first highway patrol pulled up. "The two dudes who came out to meet us didn't exactly look like Boy Scouts, did they?"

"Let me handle this." He caught a strand of her hair. "I'll tell them you didn't see anything, never left the truck. Okay?"

"Do you think they'll want to question me?"

Leaning forward in his seat, he pulled his ID and badge from his pocket. "Not when I show them this. As soon as I make it clear we don't know anything, they'll let us go. Then we can continue on to Zeke's place. The sooner we raise the alarm with him, the better."

She nodded and released the handle with a snap.

Shading his eyes, Rob marched up to the first patrolman and explained the situation. He ended by crossing his arms and saying, "Looks like the guy was shot, close range."

Another patrolman called from the wreck, holding up a bag. "Drugs."

Rob swore under his breath. EGV's people must keep a supply on hand to implicate unsuspecting and innocent people...and dead people.

The patrolman in front of him cracked a smile. "Looks like you boys might be getting this case anyway."

"Maybe so." Rob jerked his thumb over his shoulder. "Can we be on our way now? You have my card if you need anything else, and like you said, we might be picking this up anyway."

"Yeah, sure." The patrolman stuck Rob's card in his front pocket and pivoted back to the scene.

Rob strode back to the truck and climbed into the cab. "That was easy."

"Professional courtesy?"

"Something like that." He cranked on the ignition. "Also, they found drugs in the trunk."

Libby covered her mouth. "Just like me. They want to make sure to blame the victim, don't they?"

"Blame the victim, muddy the waters, divert suspicion from the real motive. I hope Highway Patrol does throw the case to us. Then I can set things right for Troy. He deserves that."

"Rob?" Libby was turned around in her seat.

"What is it?" He shifted his gaze to his rear-view mirror as they made a dip in the road.

"I saw some lights behind us. C-could that be the highway patrol following us?"

"No way." He squinted into the mirror and caught a flash of something coming over the rise. His foot came down hard on the gas pedal, and his V-8 roared.

Libby braced a hand against the door. "What is it? Is there someone behind us?"

"Someone who just cut their lights."

She whipped around in her seat again. "Why would someone drive without lights in the middle of the desert? I don't care how deserted it is, nobody would do that."

"Unless they didn't want to be detected."

"Rob, are you saying we're being followed? How? Why would they think we're out on this stretch of highway? They don't know anything about that campsite, or they would've paid it a visit by now to collect my phone."

Gripping the wheel, Rob tipped his head back and swore. "They have Troy's phone."

"So what? I didn't tell Troy where the phone was. They wouldn't be able to locate that site from the description I texted Troy. They may not even have the same phone with that text on it."

Rob turned off his own lights, and the darkness engulfed them. "Remember how Troy found us in Tucson after we dropped off Teresa?"

"He put a GPS tracker on your truck." Libby rubbed her arms. "What does that mean? How'd they get that GPS?"

"Libby, it's on his phone. They took Troy's phone after they killed him and found the tracking program." He pounded the steering wheel. "As soon as I learned Troy had a GPS on my truck, I should've demanded he remove it."

"C-can you find it now? Remove it now?"

"With that bearing down on us? I'm not going to take that chance with you in the truck."

She scooted forward in her seat. "We just left a gaggle of emergency vehicles back there. Can we turn around and get help?"

"We would have to drive straight back toward them. We'd have a shoot-out before we ever reached the scene of Troy's accident." Rob swallowed. "Do you know how much firepower these cartels have? I'm not bringing that to bear on those EMTs and patrolmen. There would be a slaughter."

"Your phone. I'll call the Border Patrol. You can let them know what to expect, and they can come prepared. Surely you guys can match them weapon for weapon?"

"You can try, but we usually can't get service

out here, Libby. Texts, maybe. Phone calls? Not so much."

She pounced on his phone and tapped it. Held it to the window and tapped it. "But you used your phone back at the accident site."

"To call 911."

"Can I text?"

"Not the Border Patrol."

"How about the individual agents?"

"I don't want them walking into an ambush." He clenched his teeth. This was his mess. He wasn't going to put another agent's life at risk.

Libby stashed his useless phone in the cup holder and caught his arm. "Where are we going, Rob? We can't go back to Luna and Zeke. We're not bringing that to rain down on them, either."

"I agree. We need to get out of this on our own." His foot eased off the accelerator.

"What are you doing? It's time to speed up, not slow down."

"I can't take the next turn at this speed. We'll flip."

"Next turn?"

As he cranked the wheel to the left across the oncoming lane of traffic, the tires squealed and Libby's body fell against his arm. "Sorry. You okay?"

"I'm not okay, Rob. Where are we going?

They're tracking us via Troy's GPS. We don't have a chance."

"We can do this, Libby. You just have to trust me. Can you do that?"

"I've done that from the minute you picked me up in the desert—or at least from the minute I dropped my knife."

"We're ditching the truck."

"Wait—did I just say I trusted you?" She pressed the heel of her hand against her forehead. "Are you out of your mind? Once we ditch this truck, they won't be able to track us anymore but we'll be on foot. In the desert. In the middle of the night."

"C'mon. You've been there, done that." Rob leaned over the steering wheel. He wanted to ditch the truck but not crash it into a saguaro cactus. "Besides, as you pointed out, they can't track us without the truck."

"Why would they want to? They'll just find a couple of corpses."

"We still have a head start. They kept their distance because they had the GPS." He aimed the truck off the access road and toward a gully in the sand. "At the bottom of this dip, we abandon the truck and get out."

"Could we maybe search for the GPS on the truck first, remove it and get back in the vehicle…where it's safe?"

"This truck is not safe. It's a big target, although I'm glad it's black, and we don't have enough time to look for the GPS. Can't do it in the dark, and can't put the lights on." He halted the truck and cut the engine. "It's go time."

"It's go crazy time." She hung on to her seat belt strap as if daring him to pull her out of the truck. "I thought I was the one with holes in my mind."

Rob reached into the back seat and grabbed his backpack. "I didn't leave home without my bag of tricks because I didn't know what we'd find when we picked up your phone. Who knew we'd need it to…?"

"Survive, right? This is do or die?"

He hauled the backpack into the center console and kissed Libby's mouth. "It is. Let's get moving."

This time he was glad she didn't wait for him to get her door. She scrambled out of the truck and eased it closed.

Reaching into his backpack, he said, "I brought a weapon for you. It's the one you had at my house when I left you alone with Teresa. Can you handle it?"

"Point and shoot. I'd rather have it than not." She patted the front pocket of her jeans. "I have my knife, too."

He grabbed her hand. "Follow in my steps.

Even though I have a flashlight in my bag, I don't want to use it out here. We shouldn't use the lights from our phones, either."

"Won't they be able to follow our footsteps in the sand?" She glanced down at her own feet creating divots in the sand.

"Maybe they will, but it won't be easier than following a GPS… And I have a plan."

"That's good to hear. What is it? We must be close to the border."

"We are. That's why we're here. I know this terrain better than they do."

She huffed behind him. "There are snakes and tarantulas and other…things out here, aren't there? I got a look at a few of them after the accident."

"The most dangerous animal out here right now is the one coming for us, and you'd better believe nothing's going to stop him." Rob cranked his head over his shoulder. "If they've realized we've gone off-road, they know we're on to them."

"And they don't have to get out of their vehicle. They'll reach us faster now. Where are we headed? We can't hide out in the middle of the desert all night. I tried it."

"We're not going to be in the middle of the desert. We're going right there." He pointed to a ridge and some scrubby desert bushes.

"That doesn't look very promising to me." She leaned her head on his shoulder, her breath coming out in short spurts.

"You're not supposed to be able to see it, and neither are they." He adjusted his backpack. "It's a tunnel, Libby, a tunnel that runs beneath the border."

"A tunnel? The tunnel where my mother was murdered?" Libby spun around in the sand, falling to her knees. "I can't do it, Rob. I can't go in there."

Chapter Nineteen

The sand and grit dug into her palms as she tried to push up to her feet. She couldn't—and she couldn't crawl into a tunnel, which had been the last thing her mother had done.

Rob dropped to the ground beside her. "It's not the same tunnel, Libby. We've closed all of those. We had three left to cut off, and this is one of them."

"I don't think I can, Rob."

"Your mother would want you to survive, wouldn't she? It sounds like she did everything she knew how to do to help you at the end. Don't waste that."

Libby sat back on her haunches and brushed her hands together. "Lead the way."

"First we're going to try to cover our tracks around here. Shuffle around in the sand from side to side."

They spent a few precious minutes scuffing through the sand to cover their footprints.

Rob braced his foot against a rock. “Now, follow me. We’re going to hop from rock to rock to the entrance of the tunnel. We’re gonna have to crawl on our bellies to get in, but if I recall, this particular tunnel is paved and we’ll be able to stand to our full height—or you will be.”

Rob jumped to the first rock and held out his hand to her. “As soon as I leave this rock for that clump of brush, take my place. Our stepping-stones don’t have to be literal stones. There’s scrubby brush we can use, too. Any hard object in the sand that’s not going to show a footprint.”

Like a couple of kids playing hopscotch, they jumped and careened and stepped from spot to spot toward that dark ridge that seemed to forecast her doom.

At the last anchor, she froze. “Rob, I hear an engine.”

“I’ve been hearing it. They’re on the way.” He curled his hand. “C’mon. One more and then we hit the ground.”

“Okay, I’m ready.” She jumped toward Rob and he caught her, wrapping his arms around her. She wanted to stay here and forget about the men coming for them, forget about the tunnel at their feet.

“We’re gonna crouch down here. The entrance is between those two rocks. It’s big enough for a grown man to get through, so you won't have any problems." He placed his hands on her shoulders. "You can do this, Libby. I'll be right behind you."

"Behind me?" She gulped. "You mean I have to go through first?"

"I'm not crawling in there and leaving you out here by yourself. You'll be safe inside. Hurry."

Libby bent her knees, which felt stiff as boards. From above, Rob guided her. No wonder the cartels and coyotes got away with these tunnels. She was kneeling right in front of the opening and still needed Rob to tell her how to get inside.

As Libby crawled into the tunnel, she thought about her mother doing the same thing over a month ago. She whispered into the darkness, "Why, Mom?"

After several seconds of claustrophobia where she felt the dirt walls closing in on her, she took a breath that didn't result in grains of sand in her mouth. Her hands no longer scrabbled through dirt, but hit smooth cement.

Rob slithered through the entrance behind her, bumping her back with his head. "Is that you?"

"It had better be." Still on her knees, Libby stretched up. "There's a lot of room in here. I can't believe it."

"You'd be surprised at some of these tunnels." Rob crawled past her and sat up. "Can you stand?"

Holding her hands above her head, she rose to her feet. "Almost. Can we use the light from our phones in here, or will they see?"

"They won't see a thing from inside this tunnel."

Libby grabbed her phone from her purse and turned on the flashlight. She scanned Rob's face first, just to make sure he was beside her. "We made it. Now what?"

"They'll be coming after us. They might suspect we're in a tunnel, but they're going to have a hard time figuring out how to get in here." Rob tossed his backpack on the ground and plunged his hands inside.

"So, we're going to wait it out or what? They'll never give up, will they? We could cross to the other side of the border and get to a place where we can make a call from our phones."

Rob didn't answer her. He was busy pulling items from his backpack—scopes, wires, another gun, a rope.

Narrowing her eyes, she said, "We're going to use all that stuff?"

"If we hope to survive, we are." He picked up a pair of goggles. "These are night vision. We have to be able to see our enemies before we can take them out."

"T-take them out?" Libby ran a hand through her tangled hair. "We're not just going to hide? Wait for the cavalry? I didn't realize we were going to engage them."

"They will engage us. Make no mistake about it." He held a finger to his lips. "Shh."

Libby kept still, even though her insides quivered as she heard shouts from outside the tunnel.

She scooted next to Rob. "Can you hear them? Are they speaking Spanish or English?"

"They're speaking English—for my benefit. As far as I can tell, they're ordering us to come out from hiding."

"Or what?" She pulled the gun from her purse that she'd slipped in there earlier. "You tell me where to shoot, Rob, and I'll pull the trigger."

"I have no doubt about it, but don't get trigger-happy just yet."

A barrage of gunfire erupted outside, and Libby jerked back. "What are they doing?"

"Those are automatic weapons. They're shooting up the ridge. They must think they're gonna get lucky and hit us."

"Are we protected in here?"

"Stay away from the entrance and try to keep low to the ground when they're shooting."

She curled a finger around Rob's belt loop. "It doesn't sound like they'll ever stop."

And then silence descended and it was ten times worse than the bullets. "What's going on?"

Rob strapped on the night-vision goggles and did an army crawl toward the tunnel's opening, his gun clutched in his hand. He hoisted himself on top of the hunk of rock that blocked the rest of the entrance.

He aimed his thumb to the left and whispered, "They're that way. I can't make out what they're doing."

As his words ended, an explosion rocked the tunnel and threw her onto the ground. Her ears rang and she coughed up dirt.

The blast knocked Rob back, and he reached for her. "Are you all right?"

"I'm fine, but they're going to blast us out of here, aren't they? They have explosives, and they're just going to keep bombing away at us until we die or stagger out of here…and die."

"Nobody's gonna die—at least not us." He wiped dirt from his face and adjusted the goggles. "They're moving down the line. There's going to be another explosion, so brace yourself. Eventually, they'll stop in front of us—within my range."

Libby crouched on the floor of the tunnel, covering her ears. Preparing for the upcoming explosion didn't help much. This one rocked them even more than the first one. The next one would destroy the tunnel or them—or both.

When the dust settled, Rob got back into position. He murmured to himself, "C'mon, c'mon, you SOBs."

Rob's body tensed and Libby braced for the blast to end all blasts.

Instead, Rob fired off several shots. He cranked his head around, the goggles making him look like some alien desert creature. "I got 'em."

He scrambled from the tunnel, ordering her to stay behind. When he called her from outside, she wasted no time joining him.

Her jaw dropped as she picked her way over the rocks and debris outside the tunnel. Dust choked the air and filled her lungs. It looked like a war zone.

She averted her gaze from a man flung out on the ground, his silver-tipped black boots pointing toward the sky.

Rob growled, "He's dead, but this one is still breathing. I'm almost glad he is."

Libby came up behind Rob crouching beside the other man, blood pumping from a wound in his chest and bubbling from his lips, his fingers inches from a crude explosive device.

Rob shone his flashlight in the man's face and still Libby didn't recognize him. She'd never seen either of these men before that she could remember.

Rob leaned over the man, his lips close to his ear, and in a harsh whisper said, "We know El Gringo Viejo is in Rocky Point. Libby's going to be able to ID him, and it'll be all over. You should give thanks you're dying because you and your compadre there are the reason we're gonna get him. He's finished."

The man hacked, and his lips stretched into a gruesome smile through the blood. "El Gringo Viejo is gone. You'll never catch him."

Epilogue

Libby smoothed out the piece of paper that contained her drawing of El Gringo Viejo, a man she had known in Rocky Point as Ted Jessup.

The authorities didn't need her drawing now. She'd been able to tell them all about the man in the cliffside compound and his murder of Charlie Harper, or C. J. Hart, that she'd witnessed. She'd been able to direct them to the compound, and they'd conducted their raid.

But the man Rob had killed in the desert was right. El Gringo Viejo was long gone.

"You'd better watch that piece of paper, Libby, or Denali is going to snatch it." April grabbed the dog's collar and pulled him away. "Clay, teach your dog some manners."

Clay Archer whistled to Denali. "I get it. When he's doing something wrong, he's my dog, and when he's being all heroic, he's yours."

"Sounds about right." April winked at Libby.

"I'm sorry about your father, April." Libby

took a sip of wine. "I think at the end, he really was trying to make amends for working with EGV all these years. He was ready to turn him in, give him up to Troy."

"Too little, too late." April dashed a tear from her cheek. "That's my dad."

"Rob, are you making arrangements for Libby? As long as EGV is on the loose, she's not safe." Clay walked up behind Libby and squeezed her shoulder. "I'm sorry, Libby. I mean, it helps that you're not the only one who knows his identity now. You can't tell us anything about him that we don't already know, but the man might want to take his revenge."

Rob rubbed a circle on Libby's back. "Now that I've passed probation and been on the job for over a year, I'm going to take a little vacation…with Libby. I'll keep her safe, and we'll figure it out from there."

"Hawaii's not a bad place to figure things out." April swirled her wine in her glass. "Do you remember everything now, Libby?"

"Almost everything." She patted Rob's thigh. "The important stuff. My therapist, Jennifer, said the rest will come gradually. I remember my mother. I remember learning about her death. I recall going to EGV's compound to show him some art and your father meeting me. Ted, EGV, meant to kill both of us, and your father saved me."

"I'm glad." April gave her a watery smile. Then she sniffled. "And I meant it. You can keep all those clothes."

"I didn't really invite you over here to return the clothes." Libby entwined her fingers with Rob's. "I just wanted to make sure you knew what your father had done for me."

Rob kissed the side of her head, and she snuggled in closer to him.

"I can take a hint." Clay jumped up and patted his leg. "Come, Denali."

April tossed back the rest of her wine. "Don't go anywhere without telling us first. You promise?"

Libby drew a cross over her heart. "I promise."

She and Rob stood on his porch and waved while Clay got Denali in the back seat of his truck and took off.

Rob draped an arm over her shoulders as they turned into the house. "Hawaii might be far enough away."

"Then what?" She stuffed a hand in his back pocket. "I stay in paradise while you go back to Paradiso by yourself? You can't expect me to stay away from you, Rob. Not when I've truly, truly found you."

He pulled her close, possessing her lips with his. The kiss he laid on her reached her toes, and she curled them into the floor.

When he came up for air, he placed a finger on her trembling bottom lip. "Can we stop talking? I've been waiting a long time to make hot, sweet love to Jane Doe."

"Jane Doe?" She broke away from his embrace and tugged at the hem of his T-shirt, yanking it halfway up his body to reveal a washboard belly that looked as if it had been kissed by the sun. She ran her hands across his mocha skin. "Should I be jealous of this Jane Doe?"

"Maybe you should be." He yanked his T-shirt over his head and threw it over his shoulder. "When I laid eyes on her, I lost all reason, even though she pulled a knife on me."

"Jane Doe doesn't sound very good for you." Libby placed a finger on her chin and raised her eyes to the ceiling. "I think you'd be much better off with Libby James."

"What does Libby have that Jane doesn't?" Rob hooked his fingers in the waistband of her skirt and pulled her toward him.

She cupped his face in her hands and kissed his mouth. "Libby's already half in love with you."

"Only half?" He swept her up in his arms and carried her off to his bedroom. Sitting on the edge of the bed, he cradled her in his lap. "I guess I have some work to do. I plan to give you a night you'll never forget."

She sighed against his lips. "As if I ever would."

* * * * *

Look for the next book in Carol Ericson's Holding the Line miniseries when
Buried Secrets
goes on sale in September 2020.

And don't miss the previous titles in the miniseries:

Evasive Action
Chain of Custody

Available now wherever Harlequin Intrigue books are sold!